COUNTRY
LEGACY

SHIPMENT 1

Courted by the Cowboy by Sasha Summers
A Valentine for the Cowboy by Rebecca Winters
The Maverick's Bridal Bargain by Christy Jeffries
A Baby for the Deputy by Cathy McDavid
Safe in the Lawman's Arms by Patricia Johns
The Rancher and the Baby by Marie Ferrarella

SHIPMENT 2

Cowboy Doctor by Rebecca Winters
Rodeo Rancher by Mary Sullivan
The Cowboy Takes a Wife by Trish Milburn
A Baby for the Sheriff by Mary Leo
The Kentucky Cowboy's Baby by Heidi Hormel
Her Cowboy Lawman by Pamela Britton

SHIPMENT 3

A Texas Soldier's Family by Cathy Gillen Thacker
A Baby on His Doorstep by Roz Denny Fox
The Rancher's Surprise Baby by Trish Milburn
A Cowboy to Call Daddy by Sasha Summers
Made for the Rancher by Rebecca Winters
The Rancher's Baby Proposal by Barbara White Daille
The Cowboy and the Baby by Marie Ferrarella

SHIPMENT 4

Her Stubborn Cowboy by Patricia Johns
Texas Lullaby by Tina Leonard
The Texan's Little Secret by Barbara White Daille
The Texan's Surprise Son by Cathy McDavid
It Happened One Wedding Night by Karen Rose Smith
The Cowboy's Convenient Bride by Donna Alward

COUNTRY
LEGACY

A MAVERICK
AND A HALF

USA TODAY BESTSELLING AUTHOR

Marie Ferrarella

HARLEQUIN

Special thanks and acknowledgment are given to
Marie Ferrarella for her contribution to the
Montana Mavericks: The Baby Bonanza continuity.

Recycling programs
for this product may
not exist in your area.

ISBN-13: 978-1-335-52358-7

A Maverick and a Half
First published in 2016. This edition published in 2022.
Copyright © 2016 by Harlequin Enterprises ULC

For questions and comments about the quality of this book,
please contact us at CustomerService@Harlequin.com.

Harlequin Enterprises ULC
22 Adelaide St. West, 41st Floor
Toronto, Ontario M5H 4E3, Canada
www.Harlequin.com

Printed in U.S.A.

USA TODAY bestselling and RITA® Award–winning author **Marie Ferrarella** has written more than three hundred books for Harlequin, some under the name Marie Nicole. Her romances are beloved by fans worldwide. Visit her website, marieferrarella.com.

To
Megan Broderick,
Welcome to the
Fun House!

Chapter 1

All he had come in for was a glass of water.

Ranching was hard, sweaty work, even in September. Granted, if he was so inclined, he could have easily spent his days just sitting on the porch, delegating work to a myriad of ranch hands and no one would have said anything, but that just wasn't his way.

As far back as he could remember, Anderson Dalton had loved working on the family ranch, loved being one with the land as well as the animals that were kept here. Ranch work wasn't a hardship for him, but he had to admit that there were times, when he got too caught up in what he was doing, that he did wind up working up a powerful thirst.

Walking into the kitchen and wiping the sweat off his brow with the back of his wrist, Anderson made his way to the sink.

But he'd made the mistake of absently glancing toward the wall. Specifically, the wall where the old, faded off-white landline was mounted.

That was when he saw it.

The red light blinking at him like the bloodshot eye of an aging dragon way past its prime but still a force to be reckoned with in its own right.

Anderson kept the landline with its answering machine in service because out on the range cell phone signals had a habit of playing hide-and-seek with him. Not to mention he had a tendency to lose his cell phone while riding and doing the thousand and one chores that a large ranch required. Because he was now a father, he had taken to keeping one close by despite all this.

When he saw the pulsing red light, Anderson's first reaction was just to ignore it and walk out again. But a nagging voice in his head urged him to listen to the message.

You never know. It might be important.

Now that he had an eleven-year-old son to take care of—albeit temporarily—everything was different. He had to be more responsible, more cautious, more aware of things than he'd ever been before.

Fatherhood at best was a hard thing to get used to. Instant fatherhood to an eleven-year-old was a whole different ball game altogether. He'd been discovering that firsthand since this July when Lexie James, the woman he'd had a casual one-night stand with twelve years ago, showed up on his doorstep asking him to take temporary custody of their son while she "worked some things out."

Eager to finally get to know his son, Anderson had agreed without a second's hesitation. He hadn't realized that being a father demanded years of on-the-job training. It wasn't something that happened overnight. But he was trying his best.

Downing the glass of water he'd come in for in three quick gulps, Anderson crossed to the wall phone in a few long strides and hit the Play button.

"You have one new message. First new message," the machine metallically announced. The next moment, the machine's robotic-sounding voice was replaced with a very melodic one.

"Mr. Dalton, this is Ms. Laramie, Jake's teacher. We need to talk. Please call me back so we can make an appointment." She proceeded to leave Rust Creek Falls Elementary's phone number before terminating her call.

Anderson stood there, staring at the answering machine.

"We need to talk."

What the hell was *that* supposed to mean?

Anderson closed his eyes. Glimmers of déjà vu flashed through his mind, propelling him back to his own school days all over again. He'd certainly been a bright enough kid, but his mind was always wandering, going in all different directions at once, most of which were not scholastic in nature. That didn't make him the best student in the classic sense of the word.

His mouth curved a little. Obviously the son whose existence he'd only discovered a year ago was a chip off the old block.

He'd only gotten temporary custody of Jake this July and school had just been in session for a couple of weeks now. How much trouble could the boy be in? Anderson couldn't help wondering.

If it was something major—like accidentally blowing up the boys' bathroom, he thought, remembering an incident out of his own past—wouldn't Paige have alerted him? The fourth-grade class that his younger sister taught was located right across the hall from his son's fifth-grade classroom and he was fairly certain that if anything actually bad had happened, he would have known it by now. Paige would have called to tell him.

Fairly certain, but not *completely* certain.

Muttering a few very choice sentiments about thin-skinned teachers under his breath, Anderson tapped out the numbers that connected him to his sister's cell phone.

On the third ring he heard what he assumed was his sister taking his call. But before he could say a word, he heard, "Hello, you've reached Paige Traub. Between teaching a class of energized fourth graders and chasing after my two-year-old fireball, I'm too busy to answer my phone. Please leave a message. If I'm still breathing, I'll call you back."

Anderson frowned. He hated talking to an inanimate recording—so he didn't.

Terminating the call, he could feel himself getting worked up. What right did this Ms. Laramie have to judge his son? She'd only been his teacher for two weeks. How could she find fault in the kid so fast? Besides, Jake was a good kid. He didn't mouth off, didn't act out. Hell, he hardly made any sound at all. Just his thumbs, hitting the keys on the controller of those damn video games he was so hooked on.

Considering that two and a half months ago, Jake was living in Chicago and now he was here, in Rust Creek Falls, Montana, the middle of nowhere by comparison, the kid had made a great adjustment. Just what did that woman *want* from his son?

Lily!

His brother Caleb's daughter Lily was in Jake's class, he remembered. The thought hit Anderson like a thunderbolt. Maybe *she* knew what was going on.

It took Anderson a minute to remember Caleb's number—but he might as well have spared himself the trouble. He had the same results when he called Caleb as he'd had with Paige's phone, except that this time, he didn't wait for the recorded message to go through its paces. He terminated the call before his brother's message was over.

Two strikes. Now what?

This Ms. Laramie had said to call to set up an appointment but if he found himself on the receiving end of yet another answering machine recording, he knew he'd probably yank his phone right off the wall. He didn't want to risk blowing up or losing his temper.

But he couldn't very well ignore the woman, either. After all, she'd said she wanted to talk to him about Jake. She'd probably get bent out of joint if he didn't get in contact with her.

Besides, he knew he wasn't going to have any peace of mind until this thing with the thin-skinned lady teacher was resolved.

That left him only one option. School was almost over for the day, but the last class was still in session. He'd signed Jake up for after school basketball, so that gave him a little extra time. He was going to go down to that school and have it out with that woman before this thing blew any more out of proportion.

With that, Anderson stormed out of the house, the memory of every teacher who'd ever found fault with him all those years ago spurring him on.

If someone had told Marina Laramie five years ago that she would simultaneously be juggling a teaching career and single motherhood—which entailed taking care of an infant in creative ways she'd never dreamed possible—she would have said that it just couldn't happen. The very idea of doing both wasn't feasible.

Yet here she was, fifteen minutes after her fifth graders had filed rowdily out, homeward bound, and instead of contemplating a fun evening out the way she would have only a couple of short years ago, she was hovering over her desk, trying to change Sydney's rather pungent diaper as quickly as possible.

Marina sighed, shaking her head. This was not quite the carefree life she'd once pictured for herself—but even so, she wouldn't have traded this life for anything in the world.

"Lucky for you I like kids, muffin-face," Marina said, addressing her very animated daughter, who apparently hadn't yet grasped the concept of lying still. The embodiment of perpetual motion, Sydney was all arms and legs and Marina had to be vigilant to keep the five-month-old from literally propelling herself right off the desk that had been temporarily transformed into a changing station. "Even stinky ones," Marina teased as she succeeded in separating her daughter's bottom from what was now a considerably used diaper.

Moving swiftly, she cleaned Sydney off and then slipped a fresh diaper under her. The old diaper had been tightly packed into itself like an unusual origami creation.

"Are you timing me?" she asked the baby. Reacting to the sound of her voice, her daughter seemed to cock her head and stare at her with her bright blue eyes. "I'm getting better at this. Yes, I am," Marina informed her daughter with conviction. "And I'd be better still if you could find it in that heart of yours not to wiggle all over the place quite so much."

Finished, Marina quickly disposed of the old diaper and deposited it, plus several wipes she'd used, into a plastic bag that she then knotted at the top, sealing away the last of the less than fragrant odor. The janitor hadn't been by yet and she definitely didn't want to gross the man out.

"Now then, let's get you presentable again. A lady doesn't hang around in just her undies—not unless she wants to get in a whole lot of trouble. Remember that, Sydney," Marina emphasized. "Otherwise, someday you just might find yourself changing diapers in strange places, too."

Having finished redressing her daughter, Marina popped Sydney into the car seat she had set up on her desk and tightened every available strap around her daughter—just in case. She knew she was probably being overly cautious, but she didn't want to take a chance.

"When did I turn into this super cautious, neurotic woman?" Marina murmured under her breath. "I used to be so carefree."

A lifetime ago, it seemed.

When he'd turned down the hallway, Anderson had found the door to his son's classroom open. Hearing the same voice he'd heard earlier on his answering machine, he walked in, loaded for bear. He assumed that this Ms. Laramie was talking to someone, but he didn't care. He wanted her to know that he was here and that he was ready to have it out with her about whatever it was that she found so lacking in his son—and he wasn't about to go away until it was resolved.

He hadn't expected to find his son's teacher talking to a baby—or changing its diaper, either. Just how young *were* the kids in this school? he wondered.

The next beat, Anderson realized that the baby she was talking to had to be *her* baby. That in turn had him wondering just how lax things had gotten in school these days. Why would the principal allow a teacher to bring her baby in to school like it was some kind of a class project?

Didn't the woman have any money for a babysitter? Or was she checking her fifth graders out for babysitting possibilities?

In any case, all of this seemed like very unorthodox behavior to him. And this Ms. Laramie had the nerve to tell him that they had to talk about *his* son?

Anderson couldn't wait to give her a piece of his mind.

"There," Marina declared after testing the strength of the car seat straps. "That'll hold you in place, Your Majesty."

That was when she heard someone behind her clearing their throat. Startled, Marina jumped as her heart launched into double time.

She could have sworn that she and Sydney were alone. Apparently she was wrong, Marina thought as she swung around.

The next second, she blinked, not quite sure she was seeing what she thought she was seeing.

There was a six-foot-one dark-haired, blue-eyed stranger in her classroom. A stranger who looked far from happy.

Neither was she, caught like this, Marina thought, flustered as she quickly tossed the bagged diaper into the wastepaper basket. She didn't like being caught unprepared like this. She was still trying to get her bearings as a working mother and absolutely hated looking as if she was at loose ends.

"Just give me a moment," she requested, struggling to measure out her words.

She was trying to sound as if she was in control of the situation even though she was very aware of the fact that she wasn't.

Not waiting for the stranger to respond, Marina quickly hurried over to the sink where her fifth graders washed their hands whenever they got too into recess and enjoying the great outdoors.

Still flustered, Marina turned the faucet handle too quickly. The next second, she found herself on the receiving end of a water spray that promptly soaked her, if not to the skin, enough to look as if she'd been caught in an unexpected fall shower.

Even the floor beneath her feet was wet.

With a dismayed cry that sounded suspiciously like a yelp, Marina managed to turn off the water, but not before she was completely embarrassed.

She was fairly certain that the tall, dark and handsome cowboy who had just walked in, wrapped in scowling mystery, undoubtedly felt she was the veritable Queen of Klutzes.

"Sorry," she apologized, grabbing two paper towels and drying herself off as best she could. She found she needed two more just to do a passable job. Wadding up the paper towels, she tossed them into the same wastebasket that contained Sydney's diaper. "You caught me off guard."

"Apparently."

Had the word sounded any drier, it would have crackled and broken apart as it left the stranger's rather full lips.

Marina walked back to her daughter, moving the car seat closer to her on the desk before she turned fully and addressed the stranger.

In her best "teacher voice" she said to the man in her classroom, "Now then, you didn't mention your name." She spoke as pleasantly as she could, waiting for him to fill in the blank.

Anderson drew himself up to his full height, aware of just how intimidating that appeared to the casual observer.

"I'm Anderson Dalton," he informed her in a no-nonsense voice. "You left a message on my phone, saying you wanted to see me about Jake."

The name instantly rang a bell. It wasn't that big a classroom, nor that big a town, so Marina didn't have to struggle to pair up the name to a student. But she was a little mystified as to why he felt the need to come in so quickly.

"Well, I didn't mean immediately," she told him, sounding half apologetic if she'd conveyed the wrong impression. "I wanted you to call me back so that we could set up an appointment for a time that was convenient to both of us."

His wide shoulders rose and fell in a careless shrug. Okay, maybe he'd gone off half-cocked and misunderstood. But all that was water under the bridge in Anderson's opinion.

"Well, I'm here now," he pointed out needlessly. "We might as well get to it—unless you want to take some time to dry off some more or maybe change your clothes," he suggested.

She didn't have a change of clothes here. It never occurred to her that she might wind up taking an unexpected bath.

"No, I'm fine."

That was Anderson's cue. He immediately launched into a defense on his son's behalf.

Taking a step closer to the teacher, he all but loomed over her as he began his rapid-fire monologue. "Look, Jake's a good kid, but you've got to remember, he's dealing with a lot right now. It's not easy for a kid his age to go from a big inner city to the sticks. Even so, I think he's doing a pretty bang-up job of it, all things considered. A lot of other kids in his place might have acted out. You just have to cut him some slack, that's all," he told her with feeling.

Marina opened her mouth but again, she didn't get a chance to utter a single word. Jake's father just kept on talking.

"If anything's wrong, then it's my fault. Jake and I hardly had time to exchange two words since I found out about him and bang, suddenly I'm the one in charge of him, making all these big decisions. And hell—heck," he censored himself, casting a side glance toward her infant daughter, "I don't know what I'm doing most of the time. This parenting thing is really tough."

Well, that's putting it mildly, Marina couldn't help thinking. But being a private person, she kept that sentiment to herself. While she was generally friendly and outgoing, there were parts of her life that she considered to be private. Her unexpected entry into motherhood was one of them.

Anderson didn't notice the silence. He kept his monologue going.

"Don't punish the kid because of my mistakes," he implored, growing more emotional. "Whatever Jake did that got you angry, he didn't know any better. Let me talk to him—"

This could go on for hours, Marina realized, dismayed.

"Mr. Dalton, stop!" she cried, raising her voice so that he would finally cease talking and take a breath. "I don't know what gave you the impression that Jake's done something wrong, but he hasn't. You've really got a great kid there, Mr. Dalton."

Anderson stopped dead and stared at her, clearly bewildered. "I don't understand," he finally said. "You said we had to talk."

"And we do," Marina agreed. One hand on the car seat, she glanced at her daughter. Despite the man's verbose monologue, Sydney appeared to be dozing. *Thank heavens for small favors,* Marina thought. "But not because he's done something bad."

The temporary relief Anderson felt quickly gave way to annoyance. "If he hasn't done anything wrong, then why am I here?" he wanted to know. "I've got a ranch to run."

She saw that if she wanted to make any headway with Anderson Dalton, she was going to have to speak up and speak with conviction. Otherwise, the man gave every impression that he would steamroll right over her and keep on going.

"I asked to see you because I am a little concerned about Jake," she told him.

In the corner of her eye, she saw Sydney beginning to stir.

Please go on sleeping, pumpkin.

"Concerned?" Anderson echoed. Was she doing a one-eighty on what she'd said a minute ago? Just what was this Ms. Laramie's game? Didn't the woman know how to speak plainly? "What's there to be concerned about?"

The man was beginning to irritate her. Marina started to wonder if this so-called meeting was ultimately an exercise in futility. But as he'd already said, he was here and since he was, she might as well press on and hope she could get through what appeared to be that thick head of his.

Sounding as friendly as possible, Marina asked, "Have you noticed how quiet Jake is?"

Anderson's eyebrows drew together in what amounted to a perplexed scowl. "Well, yeah, sure. I noticed. Why?"

Obviously the man needed to have a picture drawn for him. She did what she could to make that happen. "I'm worried that your son might be holding back something that's really bothering him."

Anderson shrugged again. *Just like a woman*, he thought. *Seeing problems where there weren't any.* Couldn't she just appreciate the fact that Jake wasn't some loudmouth class comedian?

"Jake's been quiet for as long as I've known him." Which was technically the truth. It was also a roundabout way of avoiding stating outright that the length of time he'd been acquainted with his son could only be deemed long in the eyes of a fruit fly. "Like I said, it's been a major adjustment for him—for any kid," he stressed, "to move from the city to the country. Did you ever think that maybe Jake's so quiet because he hasn't had any time to get to know all that many people here yet?"

Sydney began to fuss in earnest and Marina automatically rocked the car seat to and fro, mentally crossing her fingers as she tried to lull her daughter back to sleep. She would much rather have turned her full attention to Sydney instead of talking to a thickheaded rancher who didn't seem to know the first thing about the son living under his roof, but that wasn't her call. She was Jake's teacher and she owed it to the boy to help him if he did indeed need any help.

She tried again, tiptoeing diplomatically into the heart of the subject. "Mr. Dalton, I apologize if I sound as if I'm getting too personal here." She saw him raise an eyebrow as if he was bracing himself. "But do you and Jake ever really...talk?" she asked, emphasizing the last word.

"Sure we talk," Anderson retorted quickly, even as he thought that this wasn't any of this teacher's business. "We talk all the time."

Marina was highly skeptical about his reply, even though she had a feeling that as far as this man was concerned, he and his son actually *did* communicate.

She paused for a moment, taking a breath. She knew that she needed to tread lightly here. She didn't really know the man, not like she knew the parents of a great many of her other students, and she got the feeling that he wasn't happy about the question she was putting to him. Even so, this needed to be asked and she wasn't one who backed away, not when there was a child's well-being at stake.

"No, Mr. Dalton, I mean talk about things that really matter," she stressed.

Judging by the expression on his face, Marina felt she had her answer before the man opened his mouth to say a single word. But she waited for him to say something in his own defense anyway.

"Maybe not so much," Anderson finally conceded rather grudgingly. He didn't like having his shortcomings placed on display like this. "But I don't want Jake to feel as if I'm pressuring him about anything," he added quickly—and truthfully. He remembered what it was like, being hauled out on the proverbial carpet by one or both of his parents and taken to task for something he'd done—or hadn't done when he should have. He didn't want to make that sort of a mistake with Jake. He wanted Jake to feel like his own person.

He watched as Jake's teacher pressed her lips together and murmured, "I see."

With his back up, he felt his shoulders stiffen. *What a condescending woman*, he thought. How the hell could she possibly "see" when she knew nothing about him, about Jake or about the dynamics of their still freshly minted relationship?

"No," Anderson informed her angrily, struggling to hold on to his temper, "you don't."

The man clearly had a chip on his shoulder now, Marina thought. He hadn't behaved as if he had one when he'd first walked in. Was she somehow responsible for the change in attitude?

"All right," she conceded, giving him the benefit of the doubt. "Then why don't you tell me?"

That was *not* the response he'd expected. Caught off guard and unprepared, Anderson started talking before he had a chance to fully weigh his words.

"For the first ten years of Jake's life, I didn't even have a clue that the kid existed—so I wasn't able to be part of that life," he added, which was, to him, the whole point of his frustration. He should have been there for the boy. To guide him, to support him and to get to know him. "Now that I've gotten temporary custody, I think that Jake's confused and conflicted—not that I blame him," he added quickly. "His whole world has changed and he's discovered that everything that he thought he knew, he really didn't."

He blew out a breath and for a moment, Marina had the impression that he wasn't really talking to her anymore, but to himself—and perhaps to the boy who wasn't there.

"I really regret all those years that I lost because a kid really needs his father."

Marina felt as if she'd taken a direct blow to her abdomen. For just a second, she remembered the disinterested look on Gary's face when he told her that if she wanted to have this baby, she was on her own—as if he'd had no part in it.

The sentiment that Mr. Dalton had just expressed hit far too close to home for her to simply ignore or silently accept.

She did her best not to sound too defensive as she responded to his assessment. "Sometimes, Mr. Dalton, that just isn't possible."

Chapter 2

The moment she said the words, Anderson realized his mistake. He really needed to monitor his thoughts before he allowed them to escape his lips, Anderson upbraided himself. He could see that he'd inadvertently hurt the woman. He glanced down at the baby in the car seat. The baby's father wasn't in the picture for some reason and Ms. Laramie had obviously taken his words to heart as some sort of a rebuke when nothing could have been further from the truth.

Anderson felt a shaft of guilt pierce his ordinarily tough hide. He didn't want Jake's teacher to think that he was criticizing her.

That hadn't been his intent when he'd stormed into her classroom. He'd only been trying to defend his son.

"I'm sorry, Ms. Laramie," Anderson said contritely. "I meant no disrespect."

Marina flushed. Of course he hadn't. Why was she being so sensitive and overreacting this way? It was her job to think like a professional, not to turn everything around and focus exclusively on herself. Hormonal teenager girls did that, not state-licensed teachers.

She had to remember that, Marina silently lectured herself.

"None taken, Mr. Dalton," she replied stoically.

"Anderson," he prompted, correcting the petite redhead.

Since they'd just been talking about the ideal parenting situation, the unexpected insertion of his given name threw her. Marina looked at him, puzzled. "Excuse me?"

"Not Mr. Dalton," Anderson told her. Mr. Dalton was his father, Ben Dalton, a respected lawyer. He was just plain Anderson, a rancher. "Call me Anderson."

She'd just met him today and she wasn't accustomed to being so friendly with her students' parents if she didn't really know them outside the classroom.

"I don't think that's appro—"

"If we're going to help Jake," Anderson said, interrupting her, "I think we should be a team, not two polite strangers who sound as if they can't wait to get away from one another."

Marina frowned slightly. Was that the message she was getting across to Jake's father by addressing him formally? she wondered. That had definitely not been her intention.

"All right," she allowed, willing to do it his way. She resumed the point she'd been trying to make earlier. "Regarding what you said previously, Anderson, in a perfect world, every child would be raised by two loving parents."

Without meaning to, she glanced down at her daughter and felt a pang. Sydney was the perfect infant and she deserved to be loved by a mother *and* a father.

I'm so sorry it didn't work out, little one. But it's not all bad. I grew up without a dad, too—mostly—and things worked out for me.

"But the world, as we both know," Marina continued telling Jake's father, "is far from perfect. *Very* far."

He certainly couldn't argue with that, Anderson thought.

"True," he agreed. "I'm very aware that not every relationship can work out." Painfully aware, he thought. "But that isn't an excuse not to be there for your kid. They weren't asked to be born, but they were. The way I see it, the people who caused that birth to happen owe that kid something." He was referring to himself, although he didn't say it out loud.

Marina found herself in complete agreement with Jake's father. She also found herself wondering what had happened in Anderson Dalton's relationship that was so traumatic that his girlfriend wouldn't even notify him for ten whole years that they had had a child together.

It was on the tip of Marina's tongue to ask, but she knew that it wasn't any of her business and it had no bearing on her teacher/student relationship with Jake.

Besides, even if she was brash enough to ask Anderson about it, it might just put the man's back up. She had to remember that the point of talking to Jake's father in the first place was to get him to build a stronger relationship with his son, not satisfy her innate curiosity.

Her whole supposition about the relationship—or lack thereof—between Anderson and Jake's mother was truthfully based on her thinking that the former was a nice guy. At least, he seemed that way to her, but then she wasn't exactly the reigning authority when it came to reading men. When she came right down to it, Marina silently admitted, she didn't just have a poor track record with men, she had an absolutely horrible one.

Gary Milton was a case in point.

She'd been utterly, completely and madly in love with the man who was Sydney's father, convinced beyond a shadow of a doubt that he was The One despite the fact that they hadn't been dating all that long. At twenty-seven, with all of her friends getting married and starting families, she was more than ready to take the plunge to happily-ever-after and she was certain that Gary was, too.

Her own parents had long since been divorced, with her father hardly ever turning up in her life, but she was convinced it would be different for her and Gary.

Vulnerable, eager, she'd felt that all the stars were perfectly aligned for something wonderful to happen that July Fourth night when she and Gary had attended Braden and Jennifer's big bash of a wedding. Indeed, romance was in the air and, unbeknownst to her and most of the guests, a spiked glass of punch—thanks to party prankster Homer Gilmore—was in her hand.

What came afterward seemed completely natural at the time—almost like destiny. She and Gary came together in every sense of the word that night.

She'd expected, thanks to the night they'd spent together, to hear a proposal from Gary. But she didn't. Holding her breath, she watched the weeks go by, but Gary was no closer to popping the question than he had been before their friends' wedding celebration. And then she'd discovered that she was pregnant, and a small part of her had thought that now, finally, Gary would step up. But she was sadly mistaken.

Gary not only didn't step up, he stumbled backward and completely freaked out.

Stunned by his initial reaction, Marina had been struck utterly speechless when Gary had actually accused her of engineering her pregnancy so that she could trap him into marrying her.

Angry, Gary had loudly proclaimed that he was way too young to be "saddled" with a wife and kid. He'd broken off their relationship then and there.

An entire spectrum of feelings had gone careening through her at Gary's declaration of independence, but she'd gone positively numb when he had gone on to tactlessly suggest that she "take care of the problem."

The problem.

As if the tiny being growing inside her was anything other than a miracle, she'd thought.

That was when it had hit her with the force of a two-ton truck. She'd been wasting her time and her heart on a self-centered lowlife, foolishly thinking that this poor excuse for a human being was her Prince Charming. He didn't even qualify to be a frog prince. She'd countered his suggestion by telling him in no uncertain terms to get lost.

And he did.

So completely lost that after Sydney had been born, he'd never come by to see his daughter even a single time.

His loss, Marina had silently declared, and from that point forward, she'd eliminated all thoughts of Gary, all memories of their time together, from her mind. She had better things to do than to spend even a single moment reliving the past, or pining for a future that wasn't in the cards.

And while she was actually eternally grateful that their paths had crossed long enough to gift her with the greatest present of her life—

her daughter, Sydney—at the same time, the whole traumatic interlude with Gary had definitely scarred her. In a nutshell, it had shaken her faith in her own ability to know whether or not a person was actually a decent human being or just a deceptively charming rat on two legs.

In his own way, Gary had taught her one hell of a lesson.

"Ms. Laramie, is something wrong?"

At the sound of Anderson's deep voice, Marina roused herself. She realized that she'd allowed her thoughts to take her attention hostage, which was, as far as she was concerned, completely inexcusable behavior.

Clearing her throat, she flushed. "What? No, nothing's wrong. Sorry, something you just said started me thinking." Which was true, but undoubtedly not in the way that Anderson might have thought. So before he could ask her any further questions, she quickly redirected the conversation. "I agree with what you said."

"Great." The enthusiasm went down a notch as he asked, "What part?"

"The part about you not wanting Jake to feel as if you were pressuring him," she told him, glad that Anderson was at least partially intuitive. "Being pressured definitely wouldn't help bring your son out of his shell."

"What would?" he asked, curious to hear her take on the matter.

The blanket covering Sydney's legs slipped and she moved it back into place. Her daughter, mercifully, went on dozing but she knew that wasn't going to last for long. She needed to wrap up this conversation. "I was thinking along the lines of some TLC."

"TLC?" Anderson repeated quizzically.

Marina nodded. "That stands for tender loving care," she explained.

"I know what it stands for," he retorted, insulted. Did she think he was entirely backward and clueless? "What I'm trying to figure out is how would I go about expressing that? Are you telling me you think I should hug him and stuff?"

She hadn't been thinking along those lines, but she gave it some thought now. "An occasional hug wouldn't hurt," she acknowledged, then qualified her answer. "But in general, eleven-year-old boys aren't really into that. They're not big on that sort of parental display of affection. At least not on a regular basis."

"Then what?" Anderson asked impatiently. "I've already got him signed up for some after school sports activities," he said, "so that Jake can be around other kids participating in some bonding sports."

"All that's good," Marina agreed tentatively, not wanting to shoot down the man's fledgling enthusiasm so early in the game. "But I was thinking of something along the lines of a more personal, fulfilling activity."

He looked at her uncertainly. He wasn't sure just what she was suggesting. So far, they just seemed to be going around in circles. "Just what is it you have in mind?"

Since she wasn't sure how open he would be to her suggestion, Marina proceeded with caution. "How would you feel about Jake helping me after school a few days a week?"

Anderson had a feeling that her question wasn't as straightforward as it sounded, so he tried to get her to clarify it. "You mean like cleaning paintbrushes in the art room and stuff like that?" he asked.

Marina shook her head. "No. Jake's a sensitive, caring boy. Those sort of traits should be nurtured," she told Anderson. "I was thinking that Jake might make a perfect mother's helper."

"A mother's helper?" he repeated uncertainly, somewhat stunned and taken aback. "Isn't that something that, you know, *girls* usually do?" he asked, wondering if he should be insulted on Jake's behalf. Just what was she saying about his son?

Marina was quick to set Anderson straight. The man was stereotyping and she couldn't allow that to get in the way of Jake's development as both a student and a boy-in-progress.

"Not necessarily. All that's required to be a mother's helper is patience—and of course the desire to help. From what I've seen, Jake's equipped with both." She became more impassioned as she spoke. "There's no reason why a boy can't help out as well as a girl and I could really use a hand at home—and even here at school," she added for good measure, thinking that might help tip the scales. She was paying someone to watch Sydney while she was teaching, but she could barely afford that.

"I don't know," Anderson said after giving the whole matter less than thirty seconds of thought. "I really don't think it's a very good idea," he confessed with conviction. "Jake and I are doing okay just the way things are."

Marina banked down her growing impatience. She knew she couldn't push this. Anderson—if he *was* going to come around—was going to have to come around on his own. If she pushed in any manner, she had the distinct impression that he was the type to dig in his heels and resist until his dying breath left his body. The bottom line there was that she'd never get anywhere with him.

This way, by maintaining an open mind and an equally open door, there still might be a small chance that things would go her way. With Jake's well-being in mind, she had to take it.

She wanted to argue about it—to discuss it, actually—but the idea of arguing with the man seemed counterproductive in its own right. So for now, and the sake of peace, she went along with what Dalton suggested.

"All right," she told Anderson gamely. "But if you do happen to change your mind about this, please let me know," she requested with a large smile. "You know where to find me."

He nodded, ready to terminate the conversation. He knew the value of quitting while he was ahead.

"Just like I found you this time," he replied, already edging his way out.

Marina spoke up just as he was about to reach the door. "I just suggested Jake being a mother's helper because I think it might help him if he puts himself out in order to help someone else."

"Someone else," Anderson repeated, then knowingly added, "like you."

She saw no reason to pretend that Jake's father had guessed wrong. Marina certainly wasn't embarrassed by either the fact that she needed help nor that she would have accepted it from one of her students.

"Like me," she replied, then hurriedly tacked on, "And Sydney."

"Sidney?" Anderson questioned, suddenly lost. "Who's Sidney?"

"This lovely young lady here," Marina told him, her voice teeming with affection and pride, albeit quietly, as she indicated the car seat.

"Oh." Chagrined over his misunderstanding—and concerned about the odd sort of attraction he was experiencing—attraction to his son's teacher for heaven's sake—Anderson was practically inaudible as he mumbled, "I thought you were talking about some guy."

"An understandable mistake," she said, the corners of her mouth curving in what Anderson could only describe as an appealing smile that seemed to communicate with some inner core of his. He did what he could to block it, or at the very least, just ignore it.

"Well, it's usually a guy's name," Anderson

protested in his own defense, trying to back-track from his error.

While Marina didn't exactly contradict him, she expanded on his answer. "It's both."

She had a feeling that Jake's father was in somewhat of a combative mood and saying anything to outright oppose him would not be the smart thing to do at the moment. It fell under the heading of discretion being the better part of valor.

"Yeah, I know that," he informed her with a dismissive shrug. All he wanted to do was get out of the classroom, away from Marina Laramie and her sleeping infant. "So, if there's nothing else you want to discuss about Jake, I've got to be getting back to the ranch," he informed her, as he turned to leave. Then just before he exited, Anderson felt a need to add, "Those posts don't nail themselves up."

"I'm sure that they don't," she responded with what he had to admit seemed to him to be a very infectious grin.

He hadn't come here to make trite observations about Jake's teacher's smile, Anderson reminded himself. He'd come because he had Jake's best interests at heart and he was really trying, in his own less than stellar way, to make up for all the time that had been lost to him. Precious time he wasn't going to ever get back.

"Okay, then, so it's settled," Anderson announced as if they had arrived at a mutual agreement rather than something he was just stubbornly reiterating. "Jake's going to be playing some after school activities." Eyeing Marina Laramie, he waited for the redhead to contradict him.

But she didn't, which surprised him—as well as relieved him.

"You know what's best for your boy," she said.

"That's right," Anderson said as he strode out of the classroom, "I do."

Except that he didn't, and he knew it.

He was feeling his way around and fighting the feeling that he was doing a far from spectacular job at every turn.

Indecision nibbled away at him like a stubborn, persistent mouse. Maybe that Laramie woman had the right idea. Maybe Jake would do better helping her out after school. At least it would get him out of his room and away from those video games of his.

Heaven knew the idea of helping the woman out was not without its appeal or merits, he mused. He wouldn't mind having that job himself.

Whoa, there, Andy. Get a grip, he counseled himself. *We're talking about Jake here, not you. He's the one who could benefit from spending some extra one-on-one time with the lady.*

When he came right down to it, he didn't know why he'd turned Jake's teacher down, or why, as he left the building now, he couldn't shake the feeling of being a chastised grade-schooler. After all, the woman hadn't actually said anything to make him feel like he'd done anything wrong. If questioned, he couldn't even put his finger on one reason why he felt that way. He figured it was probably rooted deep into his past, back to the days when he actually *was* a grade-schooler and everyone was always telling him what to do.

He hadn't taken their advice then, Anderson reminded himself, and he wasn't about to start now by being led around by the nose by that slip of a redhead.

He needed to do more than that, Anderson thought as he climbed back up into his truck. He needed to keep his distance from Jake's bubbly, interfering teacher. Everything in his gut—the center of his very best survival instincts—told him that he needed to steer clear of her if he knew what was good for him and if he intended to get through this time of parental custody intact.

Not just intact, he reminded himself. He needed to do more than to remain intact. He needed to come out a winner when it came to all the matters that concerned Jake.

From the second he had found out about his son's existence, Jake was his number one priority.

As for this Ms. Laramie, the woman might be a real stunner, but she was way off base. Jake, a mother's helper? Anderson silently questioned as he now frowned at the idea. Not *his* boy, he thought. Not if he had anything to say about it.

Chapter 3

In order to terminate the awkward meeting with the fifth-grade teacher, Anderson had told her that he had to be getting back to his ranch. But instead of doing that, he decided to stick around until Jake finished playing basketball. When he thought about it, staying in the vicinity of the school made a lot more sense than driving to the ranch and then back again.

Leaving the building, Anderson got into the cab of his truck and drove around to the back entrance of the school. He told himself it was closer to where Jake would get out once basketball practice was over but to be quite honest, he wanted to be sure that Marina Laramie didn't accidentally look out the window and see him parked out in front. It would just complicate everything.

He had no idea why he put so much thought into this, but he did. For some reason, the woman made him uneasy. Avoiding her seemed the best way to go.

The moment he pulled up the brake and turned off the engine, he began to get fidgety. Accustomed to working hard from the moment he opened his eyes in the morning until he fell into bed at night, just sitting in the truck waiting had him growing progressively more restless with every passing moment.

Anderson was not a man who did "nothing" well.

He was contemplating getting out of his truck and walking around the school grounds until practice was over when the cell phone he'd thrown in the glove compartment of his vehicle—an old flip phone model—rang.

At first, Anderson didn't even hear it.

His cell phone hardly ever rang, so it caught him off guard. It took him a moment to connect the faint sound to its source of origin.

He flipped the phone open and fairly barked, "Hello?"

The annoyed greeting would have been

enough to scare a great many people away. Paige Dalton Traub was not one of those people. Younger than Anderson by five years, she was every bit as feisty as her brothers. She had to be. Having grown up with three bossy brothers and two equally bossy sisters, it took a great deal for her feathers to get even slightly ruffled. It took even more for her to become even mildly intimidated, and certainly never by a sibling.

Paige recognized her brother's less than dulcet tones immediately.

Rather than return his less than warm greeting, Paige went straight to the heart of the matter. "So, how did it go, big brother?"

Anderson had no idea what his younger sister was talking about. She might as well have been talking gibberish. Most women, in his limited experience, did.

"How did *what* go?" he countered, irritated.

Paige laughed shortly. "Ah, there's that disposition of a wet hornet that I know and love," she noted sarcastically. "You might recall that initially, you called me, and I assumed that the reason you called had something to do with Marina and your son. Am I right?" she wanted to know.

"Yes," he conceded grudgingly through clenched teeth.

"Well, I'm here now so spill it. Do you know why Marina wanted to see you, and is everything okay?"

Instead of answering her directly, Anderson approached her question from a different angle. "You told me about his teacher having a kid of her own, but you never mentioned that the woman was touchy-feely."

"She *touched* you?" Paige asked, clearly taken aback. She and the fifth-grade teacher had gotten to know one another over the last year or so and while Marina was friendly enough and everyone liked the woman, she wasn't the type to touch a student's parent.

"No," he bit off, annoyed that his sister wasn't following his train of thought. "But she wanted me to get all touchy-feely with Jake." As he spoke, his mouth curved downward into a distasteful frown. "She seems to think that Jake's too quiet."

"I should have that problem," Paige commented with a laugh. "I only wish that at least *some* of my students would be quiet like Jake." After a slight hesitation she asked, "So how did she suggest you do it?" When he didn't say anything, she prodded him a little. "How did she suggest you get closer to Jake?"

He frowned so hard he thought she could literally hear it in his voice as he said, "She asked me for permission to turn Jake into a mother's helper. Isn't that just crazy?" he wanted to know, assuming that his sister would have the same sort of reaction to the other woman's idea that he did.

Paige took him totally by surprise when she replied, "Actually, Anderson, I think that might not be such a bad idea."

It took him a second to collect himself and recover. "What? Is this some kind of a woman thing?" he asked, stunned.

"Only in the sense that women are more intuitive than men," Paige replied brightly, no doubt knowing that her remark would get to him. "But seriously," she continued, the humor fading from her voice, "I think that maybe Jake might be a little too isolated. I've been keeping an eye on him at school and I don't see him interacting with the other kids during recess."

Anderson wondered how long she'd been holding off saying anything to him. Apparently today was the day to tackle the subject.

"He's a sweet kid," she continued, "but he needs to acquire some people skills, Anderson.

To that end, I think it might do him some good to take care of another person instead of just being aware of his own small sphere."

"Well, it's not like he's going to go backpacking on some survivalist's journey, fending for himself and that baby," Anderson retorted. He felt disappointed. He'd expected Paige to be on his side, not playing for the opposition. "Jake would be taking care of that baby under this Ms. Laramie's supervision the whole time—at the very least. You can't tell me that she won't be watching Jake like a hawk the entire time."

"Not necessarily. I think that the whole point would be to give Jake the assignment, exercise a little supervision and then step back to see how he does."

Anderson banked down the urge to laugh at his sister's naivety. "Would you step back if this was you we were talking about and the baby you were leaving with someone was Carter?"

Again Paige didn't answer him the way he thought she would. "If I trusted them to look after my son and felt that I had made myself perfectly clear in my instructions, then sure."

He didn't believe it for a minute. "Well, I'm not as naive as either you or your Ms. Laramie," he informed his sister. "You don't just hand over babies to other babies and expect everything to go off without a hitch."

Paige wanted to move on to the topic that really had her interest, but she knew that she needed to get her ordinarily calm brother back to that state before she could go on. Ever since Jake had moved out here, it was as if she didn't even recognize her oldest brother. Anderson had become a different person. A completely uptight, unsettled, different person who seemed to be perpetually afraid of making the wrong move.

"Jake isn't a baby, Anderson. He's halfway to becoming a man—"

Anderson quickly cut her off. "Not for another ten years."

He didn't believe that, did he? "A lot sooner than that," Paige contradicted. "You might as well get used to the idea. Anyway, I didn't call you to discuss Jake's so-called fragile masculinity—or yours," she added. "I called to find out something else."

"What?" he all but snarled. He didn't feel that he could take on another problem right now.

For the second time since she'd called, his sister caught him off guard when she asked, "What did you think of her?"

"Her?" Confusion all but throbbed in his voice. What was Paige talking about?

"Marina Laramie," Paige said patiently.

Why was his sister asking him something like that? "I guess that she's an all right teacher," Anderson finally conceded, thinking that was what he was being asked.

"No." Paige tried again. "What did *you* think of *her*?"

"Think of her?" Anderson echoed, at this point thoroughly confused by Paige's tone as well as her question.

Paige sighed. Men could be so thick, she thought. "This isn't brain surgery, Anderson. Or a trick question," she added in case that was going to be his next guess. "It's really a very simple question," she stressed.

"It's not a simple question," Anderson contradicted. "It's a prying, complex question. What did I think of her?" he repeated, then before she could make any sort of a remark or reply, he continued by asking her a question of his own. "In terms of what? A first-time teacher? A woman who sounds like she has trouble understanding and relating to boys?"

"As a person," Paige interjected, finally getting a chance to get a word in edgewise. "What do you think of Marina Laramie as a person?"

"Why?" Anderson asked suspiciously. It had taken a while before the red flags had gone up for him, but they were flapping madly in the wind now. "Just what is it that you're trying to cook up in that scheming little head of yours?" he wanted to know.

"I'm not 'cooking up' anything," Paige protested. "I wasn't the one who asked you down to the school for a conference, Marina was. I just thought that…well, now that you've seen her and since you were single and she was single…"

Okay, this had gone far enough, Anderson thought. He needed to stop his sister before she *really* got carried away.

"One and one don't always make two, Paige," he ground out.

In her opinion, one and one *always* made two. "You never know until you try," Paige stressed.

"Oh, I know, all right. Trust me, I know," he told her in no uncertain terms. "Besides, I'm not looking for anything—or any*one*."

She already knew that and she thought it was a terrible waste for her oldest brother to be alone like this. "But if you stumble across it right out there in your path—" Paige began.

"I don't plan to do any stumbling, either," Anderson informed her tersely.

As far as he was concerned, one mistake was more than enough for him. Not that he'd actually had any ideas about a possible relationship blossoming between Lexie and him twelve years ago. It had been just one of those classic things, an enjoyable fling that lasted the span of one night, no longer. And, after dealing with the woman, he realized just how fortunate he was *not* to have wanted any sort of a relationship with Jake's mother. They didn't have very much in common.

Now that he thought about it, he wasn't the kind of guy who did well when it came to relationships. Hardworking and blessed with common sense, Anderson knew his shortcomings and he wasn't looking to get involved with anyone.

Even so, it was obvious to him that his sister had other ideas. He needed to set her straight once and for all.

"Look, kid, I realize that you think that since you have this great thing going with Sutter everyone should be married, but it's just not like that for some of us. I'm glad you found somebody to love you, someone who lights up your world, but that isn't my destiny and I'm okay with that."

But apparently Paige was not about to accept defeat for her brother so easily.

"Just because it didn't work out for you and Lexie—her loss, by the way—" she interjected.

Anderson laughed softly. This was the Paige he was more familiar with. The sister who was fiercely loyal to the members of her family and immediately took offense on their behalf.

"Thank you. You're my sister and you have to say that."

"No, I don't," Paige contradicted. "And stop interrupting. What I'm trying to say is that just because it didn't work out for Lexie and you doesn't mean that it won't work out for you with someone else."

She just wouldn't let this go, would she? Ordinarily, he might just let this go for now, but it was far too important to let her think she'd won, even by default.

"It won't because I'm not looking for it to work out—*with anybody*," he underscored. "Look, Paige, I know you mean well, but really, let it go. I'm happy just the way I am."

Paige dug in. "A year ago, you thought you were happy just the way you were, then you found out about Jake and suddenly you wanted him to be a permanent part of your life. You still do," she pointed out, remembering how dejected Anderson had been when Lexie had denied him custody or even visitation rights.

"Don't try to confuse me with your logic, Paige." He was only half kidding.

"It's not 'my' logic," his sister pointed out. "It's just logic."

Anderson blew out an impatient breath. There was just no arguing with his sister once she got going like this. He didn't want to say something to her that he would wind up regretting, but he didn't want her thinking that she was going to emerge the victor in this argument, either.

And then the cavalry arrived in the form of a lanky eleven-year-old boy. Spotting him, Jake was striding toward his truck.

"Sorry, Paige, I'd love to talk some more, but Jake just turned up. Basketball practice must be over. Time to take him home and put him to work," Anderson announced cheerfully. "We'll talk later," he promised, terminating the call before she could say another word.

Or you'll talk later and I'll have to listen, he silently added, tossing the cell phone back into the glove compartment.

Leaning over, Anderson opened the passenger door for his son.

"Hi, how was it?" he asked Jake cheerfully. Then, just in case that sounded a little too vague to his son, Anderson clarified the focus of his question. "How was basketball practice?"

Jake slid into the passenger seat and dutifully buckled up his seat belt.

"It was okay." The reply was completely devoid of any enthusiasm.

Starting up the truck, Anderson pulled out of his parking spot, his eyes trained on the rearview mirror until he put the transmission into Drive.

"Did you play a game?" he asked in the same cheerful voice.

Settling into his seat, Jake kept his eyes forward. "Yes."

He was not exactly a conversationalist himself, but for the sake of trying to draw his son out, he gave it his best shot.

"And then what?"

"We stopped," Jake said matter-of-factly. Then, as the word just hung alone in the air, he explained, "It was time to go home."

This was not going well. "Do you like playing basketball?" Anderson prodded.

His thin shoulders carelessly rose and fell in response as he continued looking out of the front windshield. "It's okay."

That was not exactly a ringing endorsement of the sport. Maybe he'd pressured the boy into playing something he had no desire to participate in.

"Would you rather have me sign you up for something else? Baseball maybe, or football?" Anderson suggested, glancing at Jake's face for a response.

That was the extent of the after school sports activities that were available and he wasn't really sure about the baseball part. The actual baseball season, he was only vaguely aware, was over and he wasn't sure if anyone was available to coach boys in the off-season. He'd never been one to enroll in any of those sports himself when he was a kid. All he'd ever been interested in were things that had to do with ranching.

"You know, it's not a bad idea to try to broaden yourself a little bit," Anderson told his son. He hadn't been critical yet, but maybe a small bit of pressure wasn't a bad idea. "Sitting in your room all day playing video games isn't healthy."

"I don't play all day," Jake answered, finally turning toward him. "I go to school."

It wasn't a smart-aleck answer, but it didn't exactly leave room for a warm exchange. Determined to get through to Jake, he tried another approach.

"You need to socialize, Jake. To get to know people. You need to make some friends."

"Why?" Jake wanted to know. He wasn't being belligerent; he was just asking a question.

It was a question Anderson wasn't prepared for and he had no answer ready, so he fell back to an old tried-and-true response parents had used since time began. "You just do."

"Oh." Jake went back to looking out the windshield, watching the desolate scenery go by.

Maybe, Anderson thought as silence descended within the vehicle's cab, that teacher he'd seen today did have a point.

And then again, he thought rebelliously in the next breath, maybe not.

Chapter 4

"Something bothering you, Jake?"

Ever since his meeting last week with the red-headed teacher, Anderson had been more attuned to Jake's silence. All during dinner tonight his son had been even quieter than usual, but for the duration of their trip into town the boy hadn't said a single word. Anderson was taking Jake with him to the town meeting that was being held tonight and they were almost there.

Granted, his son had looked less than happy about having to make this trip when he'd initially suggested it, but he would have thought that the boy would have said *something* by now. Kids his age *talked*, if only to complain.

But Jake didn't.

Jake was really a hard kid to figure out, Anderson thought wearily.

A heartfelt, mighty sigh preceded Jake's reply when he finally spoke. "I was just about to get to the next level."

"The next level of what?" Anderson asked, puzzled.

He had no idea what his son was talking about. He and Jake shared a house and they shared bloodlines, but at times it was as if they were from two entirely different worlds. Trips to and from school might hear a word or two exchanged and mealtimes were hardly a hotbed of verbal exchange, either, if it was just the two of them at the table instead of occasionally one of his siblings.

But even so, *something* was usually said, some nominal conversation that lasted a couple of minutes. But not this time. Jake hadn't said a word from the time that he had stepped out of his room for the trip to town.

That was right after Jake had looked at him, clearly confused as to why he was going to this meeting and what he was going to do once he got there.

"I thought it might be a good idea for you to see how people in a small town get things done," Anderson had told his son.

But that was only part of the reason he was taking Jake with him. He was also trying to get the boy to feel more involved in what was going on. He was hoping that if his son felt more a part of Rust Creek Falls, he'd open up a little more.

Jake hadn't protested going to the meeting the way a lot of boys his age might have. For that matter, he hadn't dragged his heels, or thrown a tantrum, or mouthed off. Instead, offering no resistance, Jake had just silently come along—but the boy definitely hadn't looked happy about it.

But then, Jake wasn't exactly the definition of a happy-go-lucky kid to begin with.

Still, the silence had really gotten under Anderson's skin and when his son hadn't uttered a single word the whole half hour trip to the town hall, he'd finally decided to initiate some sort of a conversation. The only trouble was, once Jake had answered him, he didn't understand Jake's response.

"The next level in 'Mighty Warriors,'" Jake explained quietly.

"'Mighty Warriors,'" Anderson repeated slowly, as if tasting the words as he uttered them.

What he was really doing was stalling until he could remember exactly what "Mighty Warriors" was. He really was trying to take an interest in his son's life, but what Jake was into represented a whole new world to Anderson. A new world he was attempting to navigate without a road map or a guide.

"That's the video game I was playing when you said we had to go to this meeting."

Anderson was turning his truck into the first available space located in the large parking lot behind the town hall. Pulling up the hand brake, he turned off the engine and shifted in his seat to face his son.

"Oh. Well, you're a bright guy. You can always pick up where you left off when you play again," Anderson said with complete conviction.

Jake's expression gave away nothing, but even so Anderson got the feeling that maybe it wasn't all that easy to play this game his son was so obsessed with when Jake answered, "It's okay, Dad."

Thinking it safer to change the subject than wade through one that he knew absolutely nothing about, Anderson came around the hood of his truck and joined his son. In a gesture of camaraderie, he put his arm around Jake's thin shoulders before he began to walk toward the building.

Jake looked around as they came around to the front of the building. Since it was evening in September, a bevy of streetlights were on, illuminating the front entrance.

"It looks like there's going to be a lot of people here," Jake observed.

Anderson couldn't help wondering if that was a good thing or a bad thing in Jake's eyes. There was still so much he didn't know about this introverted boy he had fathered.

"Everyone who's interested," Anderson agreed. Which, he silently admitted, probably wouldn't have been him if this meeting had been held six months ago. He would have felt it was sufficient to have one of his siblings attend it and then report back on the highlights.

But now he was a family man—or at least he had a family to concern himself with—and that meant that he had to take an active interest in what was going on in town. Especially when it might affect Jake, just as the subject for this meeting promised to do.

He thought back to the wedding celebration that had been held last July Fourth with its unfortunate incidence of spiked punch. Apparently, possibly because of the wedding and definitely because of the punch, love had been in the air that night. Because of that, a large

number of babies had consequently joined the
population of Rust Creek Falls. Babies who
would eventually grow up into children—children who needed to be educated.

Presently, Rust Creek Falls Elementary was
too small a facility to adequately accommodate all these added children. The focus of the
meeting tonight was to determine whether the
town council should give the okay to just build
onto the existing school—or if it was wiser to
build a second school altogether.

Although Jake hadn't been part of that baby
boom, he was here now and, with any luck,
would remain that way. The boy was definitely
going to be affected by what would be decided
at the meeting.

"Everyone?" Jake repeated, still looking
around. His head was turning from side to side
as if he was a searchlight that had come to life.

Anderson thought he detected a hopeful note
in his son's voice. What was that all about?
Was Jake looking around, hoping to see one
of his classmates? A girl, maybe? If so, it was
a good sign.

"Pretty much," Anderson answered.

Jake spared him a look that could only be
interpreted as hopeful. "Like Ms. Laramie?"

The second his son asked whether or not

the woman would be attending, Anderson suddenly spotted the teacher in question approximately fifteen feet away from him, standing near the front entrance of the building—and talking to Paige.

Paige, from what he could tell, seemed to be alone. That meant that his brother-in-law was home with Carter, their two-year-old. Anderson wanted to catch up to Paige to talk about a few things, but not if it meant having to talk to Jake's teacher, too.

Since he and Marina Laramie had that less than productive meeting at the school the other week, he hadn't seen the woman or exchanged any words with her, either. But that didn't mean she'd been completely out of his mind.

As a matter of fact, the exact opposite seemed to be true. For some reason, Marina Laramie kept popping up in his head at completely unbidden times and Anderson didn't even remotely like the fact that she did. It made him feel as if he had no control over his own thoughts.

How else could he view having that woman's face suddenly appear in his head while he was in the middle of thinking of something entirely different from an interfering, feisty redhead who thought she knew how to raise his son better than he did?

Never mind that she probably did and that maybe she was even right in her estimation that Jake needed to get involved in something outside of himself. The bottom line was that Jake was *his* kid, not hers, and he would raise the boy any way that he saw fit.

Suddenly, he felt Jake eagerly tugging on his arm. "Hey, Dad, look. There's Ms. Laramie. Let's go over and talk to her."

But as Jake began to make his way over to his teacher, Anderson caught his son's arm, clearly surprising the boy, who looked at him quizzically.

"Ms. Laramie is already talking to someone else," Anderson pointed out.

Jake took another look just to be sure he was right.

"Yeah, but it's Aunt Paige. Aunt Paige won't mind," the boy insisted, shaking his arm free.

The next minute, Anderson saw his son striding over toward the two women. With his long, lanky legs, Jake had reached Marina and his aunt in a matter of a few quick strides. And, as he watched, just like that he saw his son transform from an abnormally quiet, serious eleven-year-old to an animated, bright, smiling boy who clearly had a lot to say.

"Ms. Laramie," Jake had called out before

he'd even reached his teacher. When she turned in his direction, he grinned broadly and asked, "Are you going to the town meeting?"

Marina was clearly surprised to see the boy, but she recovered with grace and offered him a warm smile by way of a greeting.

"Yes, I am," she told him.

"Me, too," Jake declared proudly. "I'm here with my dad. He thinks that it's a good idea for me to come see how people in a small town like Rust Creek Falls get things done."

Marina looked past the boy's head and saw his father coming up behind him. She inclined her head politely in a silent greeting.

Her vibrant blue eyes met Anderson's as she told Jake, "Your father's right. It's always a good idea for you to see how things work firsthand."

No doubt pleased at her seal of approval, Jake beamed. The next moment, he seemed to come to and realized that his aunt was standing right next to his teacher. "Hi, Aunt Paige."

It was obvious by Paige's expression that she was surprised by the boy's animated response to seeing her at what was, essentially, a school board meeting.

"Hi yourself, Jake. So your dad dragged you to this, huh?" she asked sympathetically, reading between the lines. She shook her head.

"He didn't drag me," Jake corrected politely, apparently not wanting to lose any of the points he'd just managed to score with his teacher. Turning to his father for backup, Jake asked, "Did you, Dad?"

Anderson found himself being drawn into this unexpected interaction against his will, but he couldn't very well not be supportive of his son. For some reason, having his teacher think well of him obviously meant a great deal to Jake.

"No," he told Marina, "Jake came right along without a single word of protest."

Which was technically true. It was only the boy's body language that indicated he didn't want to go to the meeting. That and his comment about not being allowed to reach the next level of the video game he'd been playing perpetually.

"Can we sit with you, Ms. Laramie?" Jake asked without warning as he looked at the woman with hopeful, soulful eyes.

The same eyes, Marina caught herself thinking, that his father had.

"Jake," Anderson admonished, surprised by his son's extroverted behavior, "you can't just put someone on the spot like that. I'm sure Ms. Laramie has made plans to sit with her friends." And that, Anderson hoped, was the end of that.

Except that it wasn't.

"Actually, I haven't," Marina contradicted, addressing her response to the boy. "Except for your aunt, of course. Otherwise, I didn't have any plans to sit with anyone in particular." She smiled warmly at the boy who had given her some concern. "You're welcome to join us," she told Jake.

Jake looked positively overjoyed.

Anderson couldn't remember ever seeing his son look so enthusiastic and overjoyed before.

And then it hit him.

His son had a crush on his teacher. There wasn't any other explanation for the way he was acting or why he looked as if he was on the verge of doing cartwheels. This was a completely different boy from the one he'd roused from his room earlier.

"Dad, too?" Jake asked eagerly.

Anderson was completely floored by his son's inclusion. Ordinarily, eleven-year-olds, whether they were male or female, were not nearly this thoughtful when it came to their parents. Or really anyone over the age of fifteen.

He could remember himself at that age. In comparison to Jake, he'd been a thoughtless, self-centered little know-it-all. Granted, he'd outgrown that phase a long time ago, but he'd still gone through it. Jake, however, had somehow managed to bypass all that. It made

Anderson realize just what a special, decent adolescent Jake really was.

Even so, if Marina Laramie represented Jake's big crush, he still didn't intend to be put on the spot because of it. He was about to politely turn down the whole invitation before it was even tendered to him, but then he saw a quirky kind of smile curve the woman's lips and heard Marina say, "Sure, why not? Your dad's included, too."

Then the petite redhead turned her very bright blue eyes on him and said, "You're welcome to join your sister and me—and your son—at the meeting if you like, Mr. Dalton."

She'd very deftly—and formally—put him on the spot. If he turned her down, he'd be the villain in his son's eyes. He'd been struggling too hard to be Jake's white knight to risk sabotaging himself just because it would entail spending an uncomfortable hour in the woman's company. Uncomfortable not because he had any real, concrete reason to dislike her—he'd actually begun to think of Jake being a babysitter as a good thing—but because there was something about this woman that made him feel…well, *antsy* was as good a word for it as any, he decided.

She made him strangely restless, like he

couldn't find a place for himself whenever she was around.

He knew it was an absurd reaction, but it was *his* reaction and as long as he was experiencing it, he wasn't going to be able to relax, certainly not anywhere around her.

But he supposed that not being able to relax was in reality a small price to pay in exchange for seeing his son looking so happy.

Looking like, he realized, a typical kid his age *should* look.

"Can we, Dad?" Jake asked eagerly, turning his face up to his father's.

Anderson slipped a hand on his son's shoulder in a gesture that spoke of familiarity and hopeful bonding. He reminded himself that this was all about Jake and nothing else, certainly not about him.

"Sure, son," he told Jake, "since Ms. Laramie said it was all right."

"I said it was all right, too," Paige reminded him, pretending to raise her hand like a student who was trying to catch her teacher's attention after being conspicuously ignored.

"I know, but you don't count," Anderson teased. "You're just my sister. You're supposed to say it's all right."

Paige narrowed her eyes as she gave her

brother a dismissive, reproving look. "Yeah, well, maybe I haven't read the little sister, big bullying brother handbook lately."

"Then maybe you should," Anderson suggested, a hint of a teasing smile barely curving the corners of his mouth. And then he deadpanned, "You'll have fewer slipups that way."

Jake looked a little confused and concerned at the exchange he was witnessing between his aunt and his father.

Noticing his expression, Marina placed a comforting hand on his forearm. When he looked at her, his expression making it clear that he was ready to hang on her every word, Marina told him, "They're only teasing each other. It's what brothers and sisters do," she added, thinking of her own younger sister.

"Oh." Jake looked as if he'd just been seriously enlightened. "I don't have a brother or a sister," he explained.

Marina resisted the temptation to tousle his hair. He looked so terribly serious. The boy needed to lighten up just a little.

"Maybe someday, you will," she told him.

He nodded solemnly. "Maybe."

It struck Anderson that his son sounded almost wistful as he uttered the single word.

Chapter 5

"C'mon, Dad, we don't want to be late," Jake urged, all but hopping from foot to foot as he tried to get his father to move faster.

This was a definite change in the boy, Anderson thought. Rather than sitting passively in front of his game console for hours on end, Jake had rushed through dinner and even helped put all the dishes into the dishwasher, all in an effort to get going.

Too bad all this enthusiasm involved something that he personally would have preferred not to have to deal with, Anderson thought.

"It's not like they're going to close the doors

the way they do when people are boarding an airplane," Anderson pointed out.

He was doing his best not to sound as reluctant as he felt. After last week's town meeting, where he wound up spending almost two hours sitting not next to Marina—that was Jake's place of honor—but one seat over, he'd still been close enough to be able to have the woman's perfume fill all the exposed pores of his body. It had certainly filled his head.

Even for days later, he could have sworn that her perfume was lingering on his clothing and on his person, constantly distracting him. It was as if he couldn't shake the scent of her away from his consciousness. That, coupled with his mind conducting unannounced ambushes on him, suddenly conjuring up images of the woman in his head, made him feel as if he had become the victim of a stalker.

Except that in this case, it was his own mind that was responsible for the stalking.

He needed to get a grip, Anderson told himself sternly.

What he *didn't* need was to be thrown back in with Marina Laramie again, this time in a somewhat more intimate setting than he'd been subjected to the last time.

But this was Back to School Night and considering that Marina was Jake's teacher, there was just no reasonable way to avoid spending time in the woman's company—unless he didn't attend the event in the first place.

"You sure you want to go back to school tonight?" Anderson asked, pausing in the kitchen despite his son's best efforts to get him out the front door. "I mean, you were just there this afternoon. To have to come back tonight just doesn't seem fair."

"I can handle it," Jake assured him, puffing up his chest a little.

Yeah, maybe you can handle it, but can I? Anderson couldn't help thinking in response.

By now, Jake was pacing around the room impatiently, moving closer and closer to the front door in an attempt to prod his father in that direction. "You look ready," the boy told him.

He might as well get this over with, Anderson thought.

"I guess I am, then," he replied. The words were no sooner out of his mouth than his son all but dashed out the front door, hurrying out to the truck. "And so are you, I see," Anderson muttered under his breath, following his son out.

It promised to be a long evening, Anderson thought as he got in behind the wheel of his truck.

"What are these things like?" he asked Jake once they were finally on their way to the elementary school. "These Back to School Night things," he elaborated in case he hadn't made himself clear.

"You've never gone to one before?" Jake asked, surprised.

"Never had a reason to go to one before," Anderson replied.

"Not even your own?"

Anderson thought for a moment, then shook his head. "I don't think I ever went to any back then. My teachers used to send notes home, so my parents knew how I was doing without having to go trudging down to the halls of learning in order to find out. So what's it like?" he wanted to know, getting back to his initial question.

Having been through it a total of five times before, Jake dutifully told his father what was involved. "You talk to my teacher and she tells you how I'm doing. Then she shows you some of my work."

Anderson supposed he could see the merit in that—if only it didn't have to involve Marina Laramie. "You mean like your drawings?"

"I'm in fifth grade, Dad," Jake reminded him, suddenly sounding very grown-up. "I don't spend time drawing."

Anderson suppressed a grin. Jake sounded way older than his years when he said that. "Sorry, didn't mean to insult you, old man."

Jake looked at him thoughtfully. "Maybe you'd better not say anything to Ms. Laramie, Dad. Just let her do the talking."

"Deal."

He wanted to go one better and not have to look at Ms. Laramie, either, but that was out of the question. The woman was far too easy on the eyes and he could see himself getting swept away without any effort on his part. As a matter of fact, it was going to take effort *not* to get swept away.

"Hey, Dad," Jake said suddenly, turning in his seat to get a better look at him.

Anderson instinctively braced himself. Now what? "Yes?"

"Do you like Ms. Laramie?"

He'd been braced, but he hadn't been expecting that. Jake's question came completely out of left field and caught him utterly off guard. For a second, he made no response. Was his son somehow being intuitive? Had Jake guessed that despite his best efforts, there was some sort of a strange attraction going on between him and the teacher?

Glancing at his son's eager face, Anderson told himself that he was overthinking this by a mile. Jake wasn't some brilliant, pint-size mind reader. His son was just asking a harmless question to satisfy his own budding curiosity. Maybe he even thought that if his teacher was seeing his dad, then his report card would have straight As.

Anderson did his best to sound honest. "I haven't given it much thought."

He secretly hoped he could be forgiven for taking refuge in a lie in order to avoid any immediate problems and confrontations with Jake. It was very obvious that the boy had a crush on the woman and maybe if he thought that his father liked her, too, he'd be jealous. That was a road Anderson definitely didn't want to go down.

"But if you did give it some thought," Jake pressed, not about to let the subject drop so quickly, "what would you say?" His eyes seemed to be almost dancing as he eagerly waited for an answer.

Anderson turned away and looked out the front windshield. His shoulders rose and fell in a vague, noncommittal response. "I guess she's okay."

"'Okay'?" Jake repeated incredulously. "She's not 'okay,'" he admonished. "She's great!" His voice throbbed with gusto. "She's terrific! She's perfect!"

This was where he just backed away with grace, Anderson thought.

"If you say so." That was supposed to be as far as he was going to go talking about Marina. But something seemed to egg him on. So he paused for a second, fighting his own internal reaction, and then he gave in and finally asked, "What makes her so great?"

Jake had his answer all prepared and didn't even hesitate for a moment. "Ms. Laramie looks out for everybody and makes sure that nobody makes fun of anybody else. That's important," Jake stressed.

He'd said it with such intensity, Anderson had an uneasy feeling that Jake was one of those people who would have been made fun of if his teacher hadn't put a stop to that activity.

He supposed that put him in the woman's debt, Anderson thought grudgingly. He felt stymied at every turn, but if this teacher really was championing his son's cause, he knew that he owed her. And Anderson Dalton was a man who made good on his debts.

"Then I guess she really is pretty great," he conceded.

He was rewarded by Jake flashing a wide, happy grin at him. Anderson thought it was priceless.

The next moment, Jake, looking around, needlessly announced, "We're here."

"I recognize the place," Anderson told him, deadpan.

Sitting ramrod straight, Jake scanned the area, looking somewhat concerned. "Looks like there are a lot of people here already."

"There are a lot of kids who go here," Anderson pointed out, then reminded his son, "But don't worry, they're not all here to see Ms. Laramie."

Jake brightened, flashing an almost sheepish smile. "You're right. Hey, there's a spot there, Dad," he said suddenly, eagerly pointing to the space. "Hurry before somebody beats you to it!"

If that one was snapped up, there'd be another one to take its place, but saying so to his son in Jake's present ramped-up mood seemed like an exercise in futility. Instead, he accommodated Jake and deftly swung his truck into the space—a space made somewhat smaller by a greedy 4x4 that had parked too far over to the left.

Ready to bound out of the cab, Jake was already unbuckling his seat belt before the truck even came to a full stop.

"Hold it, cowboy," Anderson called out, grabbing the edge of his son's jacket to keep him in place. "There's nothing to be gained by a few extra seconds if you get hurt grabbing them."

Chastised, Jake sat back down in his seat. "Yes, sir."

Pulling up the hand brake, Anderson turned off the engine. "Okay, *now* you can get out of the truck."

Jake didn't need anything more. He was out of the cab like the proverbial shot.

Anderson expected his son to be halfway into the building by the time he got out himself, but he was surprised to see the boy waiting for him on the first step.

"You waited," Anderson marveled as he approached his son.

Jake bobbed his head up and down. "I thought maybe you'd like to go in together."

Anderson smiled, pleased by the boy's thoughtful actions. Maybe this father thing was going to work out after all.

"I'd like that a lot," he told Jake.

The second Anderson reached him, Jake

began moving quickly again. Glancing over his shoulder, he saw that he'd outpaced his father again. "Can you walk faster, Dad?" Jake prodded.

Anderson nodded. "I can do that." To prove it, he stepped up his pace. So much so that he swiftly outdistanced his son.

Because Anderson's legs were so much longer, Jake had to fairly skip to keep up with him. Judging by his expression, Anderson estimated that the boy loved it.

Back to School Night, Anderson discovered, was basically an informal event. Parents were milling around the classroom with their fifth graders and their siblings.

There were tables lined up in the middle of the classroom displaying reports written by Ms. Laramie's students and, despite what Jake had said, there were also drawings and paintings done by the class—some of which Anderson thought were rather impressive—hanging on the walls.

"Why don't you show me your work?" Anderson coaxed his son as they wove their way in between the aisles.

"My reports are right here," Jake pointed out, drawing his father over to one of the tables. Within a couple of seconds, the boy had honed in on his folder and offered it to him.

Anderson curbed the urge to just flip through the pages. Instead, because he knew how much it meant to Jake, he went through the folder methodically, giving each page the attention it deserved. He read everything under Jake's eager, watchful eye.

Preoccupied and focused, Anderson still became instantly aware of her the moment she approached him, despite the fact that it was from behind.

"Good, aren't they?" Marina asked. The next moment, she had circled around to face him. And then she smiled at Jake, who seemed to actually *glow* right before his eyes. "Jake has a very gifted way with words." Raising her eyes to his, she said, "You should be very proud of your son, Mr. Dalton."

Anderson's eyes met hers for just a moment. The split second was almost enough to make him lose his train of thought. Exercising extreme effort was the only thing that saved him.

That and looking away.

"I already am," Anderson replied, looking at his son and smiling.

"So," Marina continued, the smile on her lips never wavering as she addressed Jake's father, "now that you're here, is there anything you want to ask me?"

Yes, why are you messing with my head? And why can't you look more like Mrs. Peabody, my fifth-grade teacher who stopped every clock she walked by? And why can't I shake off the scent of your perfume? Why do I want to ask you out when that's the worst possible thing I could do to either of us?

The questions flashed through his head in an instant. Out loud, he said, "No, can't think of a thing." And then something did occur to him. He added the coda. "Unless you can think of something that might need improving."

Jake had momentarily gone off to confer with one of the new friends he'd been making at school. Marina took the opportunity to focus on Anderson and answer his question in a low voice.

"Maybe our relationship."

Stunned, Anderson could only stare at her. "Excuse me?"

"Our relationship," Marina repeated, stressing the words even though they were hardly above a whisper. "Ever since you came storm-trooping into my classroom that day, you've been avoiding me."

"No, I haven't," he protested.

Her eyes narrowed. "I saw you crossing the street the other day to avoid walking by me," she told him.

She'd caught him dead to rights, but he wasn't about to go down without a fight.

"I haven't been avoiding you," he retorted, then lowered his voice when he realized he'd attracted the attention of one of the mothers in the room, who seemed to lean over in their direction, undoubtedly to hear better. "I haven't been avoiding you," he repeated at a much lower decibel. "I just didn't see the need to confer with you over every single little thing that Jake might have said at the dinner table."

Jake returned just then, incurring Anderson's silent prayer of thanks. The woman couldn't continue harping on this point if Jake was around to hear her—right? Okay, so he had been avoiding her and maybe that was cowardly of him, but it was definitely the easier way to go. A confrontation and all that entailed wouldn't be any good for Jake, either.

"You two talking about me?" Jake asked, a guileless grin on his thin lips as he looked from one adult to the other.

No matter what kind of feelings he had about Marina Laramie, his son's fifth-grade teacher was obviously doing the boy a world of good. Though part of him hated to admit it, she had drawn the boy out more in the last few weeks than he had on his own over the entire summer.

If this had been a competition, Marina would have been the obvious winner, hands down. He was man enough to admit that, just not out loud. He hadn't reached the point where he could say anything of the kind to her—yet.

But, if the time came and he had to, then he would. Jake meant everything to him.

"If you have no questions, nothing to share or point out, then this might just qualify as the shortest parent-teacher conference on record," Marina conceded, willing to let it go at that.

Even though she thought it would be beneficial to the boy, she was not about to force Anderson Dalton to talk to her—which he seemed no more inclined to do than he was inclined to have that in-depth conversation with his son she'd urged him to have.

"Unless you count our first one," Anderson reminded her.

A competitive, combative streak shot through her, not allowing her to take his comeback at face value.

"As far as substance goes, this was definitely

the shorter one," she informed him, her voice sounding just a little formal and reserved.

"Does that mean that we have to leave now?"

At Jake's question she looked over at the boy, whose eyes were on her, not his father. His brows were knit in sadness.

"Oh no, of course not," Marina assured him quickly. "You definitely don't have to leave. I was just giving your father a way out if he wanted to go."

Her eyes met Anderson's fleetingly. She had no clue as to what he was thinking, whether he welcomed the reprieve or not. The expression on Jake's face, however, had her continuing with what she was saying.

"Your dad's welcome to stay here, talk to the other parents, have some cupcakes," she suggested, gesturing at the plates of the dessert she'd made last night, strictly for this occasion.

"Did you make them?" Jake asked eagerly, already claiming one.

Marina tousled the boy's hair. "Every last one of them."

Jake bobbed his head up and down as he swallowed the bite he had taken. "I thought so."

"Why?" she asked, amused.

"Because they taste so good." To prove it,

Jake took another big bite of his cupcake, then grinned as he savored the taste.

"You have a natural charmer here, Mr. Dalton." Marina's eyes were laughing as she regarded her student. "I'd watch him like a hawk if I were you."

Jake, Anderson thought, trying not to stare at the woman, was the only one in his life that he *didn't* have to watch. She, on the other hand, was another story entirely.

Chapter 6

"I see you survived your first Back to School Night." The breezy observation was addressed to Anderson by his sister as Paige stepped out of her Jeep.

Anderson stopped working and frowned.

It was a Saturday morning and he was out on the range, doing one of his least favorite chores: looking for breaks in the fence and mending them. He knew he could just order a couple of his ranch hands to do it, but Anderson didn't believe in asking his men to do anything that he wasn't willing to do himself. So here he was, out under a particularly warm September sun, repairing fences.

He'd paused what he was doing when he'd heard the sound of an approaching vehicle. He'd assumed that it was Jerry, one of the hands, bringing Jake out to help him. His son had gamely volunteered his services at breakfast this morning and Anderson had thought it was a good idea. But he'd wanted to get started really early, so he'd told the ranch hand to bring Jake when the boy was ready.

But instead of his son, he looked up to see his sister Paige, who, he had to admit, was looking every bit as fit as she used to when she'd worked right alongside all of them on the family ranch.

Anderson studied her in silence for a second, then shook his head. "You come all the way out here to tell me that?" he wanted to know.

"Of course I did," she responded, tongue-in-cheek. "I'm your sister, or at least one of them," Paige amended, "and I care."

"If you care so much, sister, why don't you pick up a hammer?" Anderson suggested, holding one out to her. "Make yourself useful. I could use the help."

Instead of taking the hammer from him, Paige demurred. "Sorry, I'm afraid I won't be here long enough for that. I promised Sutter I'd meet him in town in less than an hour."

"Convenient," Anderson murmured, dropping the other hammer before getting back to work. "Say hi to my brother-in-law."

"What's gotten into you lately, Anderson?" Paige asked, being deliberately cheerful in contrast. "You didn't used to be so surly."

"Surly?" he echoed. "And here I thought I was being my usual charming self."

Following him as he moved down the fence, Paige shrugged. "Maybe you're just reacting to the stress of being a new parent," she conjectured. "You might think about getting some help dealing with Jake—just for a while until you get more used to being a dad," she added quickly in case her well-meaning suggestion irritated her brother or set him off.

Lately, she wasn't sure just how to read Anderson. His behavior had been unusual. But she'd been observing him and now she had a theory. A rather rock-solid sort of a theory, in her opinion.

Anderson glanced at her over his shoulder. "You volunteering?"

"Me?" She stared at her brother, stunned. "Sure. In the three minutes I have left over when I'm not chasing after Carter, or helping out taking care of Jamie Stockton's motherless triplets, or, oh yes, teaching a bunch of overenergized fourth graders. I was planning on using those three minutes to nap, but I can just pencil you in instead." She looked a little exasperated that Anderson didn't understand just how very busy almost all of her days were. "Of course I'm not volunteering, Anderson. I would if I could and you know that, but I'm practically sleepwalking through parts of my life as it is."

"And yet, here you are, looking in on me to see how I'm doing," he said with a touch of sarcasm. Paige was up to something, he could feel it. He just didn't know what yet. "They broke the 'sister' mold when they made you." He paused to pick up another handful of nails before continuing. "So who's this helper you're suggesting I contact to assist me over the bumpy parts of being a first-time dad?"

Paige stood behind him as Anderson hammered in the next board. "You could talk to Marina."

Anderson abruptly stopped working and stood up. Now it was starting to make sense. His sister was trying to play matchmaker.

"Marina?"

"Marina Laramie, Jake's teacher," Paige prompted cheerfully.

"I *know* who Marina is. *This* is your suggestion on who should help me navigate through the maze of fatherhood?" he asked incredulously. He really would have thought that Paige would know better than to attempt to play matchmaker or meddle in any way in his life. Obviously, he'd given her too much credit. "In case you hadn't noticed, she's not a father."

"No, but she is a first-time parent," Paige pointed out. "The two of you could pool your information, or maybe even—"

"I don't need to know how to diaper Jake," he bit off, interrupting.

"But you do need to know how to talk to him, how to reach him," Paige said emphatically. "And from what I've seen, Marina's pretty much got that covered. You could stand to learn from her."

"What are you, her publicity agent?" he asked, annoyed.

Paige ignored the sarcastic question. She wasn't about to get sidetracked. From what she—and their sister Lani—had observed, there was a spark between their brother and Jake's teacher and in her opinion, the two made a very good pair. All she had to do was make her thickheaded brother aware of that.

"Whether you realize it or not, you and she do have a lot in common," Paige insisted.

"You're both first-time parents and you're both single."

Okay, it was time to make his sister back off, he thought.

"Is that what this is all about?" he demanded, forgetting about the fence repairs for the moment. "Being single?"

"No," Paige immediately cried, afraid that maybe she had overplayed her hand. She knew how Anderson felt about someone trying to set him up. "It's about being alone in this parenting game and admitting that you need to pair up with someone who knows exactly what it's like to be in your shoes."

His frown looked as if it went clear down to the bone. "I don't want her in my shoes," he snapped. "Besides," he continued, his tone lightening just a little, "I'm not alone in this. I've got you and Lani and Lindsay helps when she's not too busy at Dad's firm, and I'm—"

Paige threw up her hands. "No one could ever tell you anything."

Unfazed, Anderson responded mildly, "That's because I'm older and smarter."

"Well, you certainly are older." It was all that Paige was willing to concede. Taking a deep breath, she forced herself to calm down. She'd learned long ago that yelling at Anderson never got her anywhere. "Seriously, big brother, Marina's very good at her job."

"I'm sure she is," he replied dismissively. Turning away from Paige, he got back to work. There was still a lot of fence mending left to do.

Paige could all but see her words bouncing off her brother's head, unheeded. But she wasn't about to give up or go away without saying what she'd come to say.

"And did you see the way Jake lit up around her at the town hall meeting?" she asked. "Every time she said anything to him, Jake positively glowed. You *had* to have seen that."

Anderson paused for a second, but he didn't get up and he didn't turn around. "I might have noticed," he allowed just before hammering in another nail. Hard.

There were times when he could get her so angry, Paige couldn't see straight. But this was important and she wanted to get her point across before she had to leave. "Look," she began patiently, "it's none of my business, but if you ask me—"

"I don't recall doing that," Anderson told her quietly, knowing damn well that his sister was going to ignore him. She was good like that, ignoring whatever she didn't want interfering with whatever point she was espousing.

"If you ask me," Paige repeated through clenched teeth, "I don't think that boy was getting the right sort of attention he needed from Lexie."

This time, Anderson did get up and turn around. He had deliberately avoided asking Jake anything about his mother. Lexie's behavior was a definite sore point for him, but he didn't want to make either his son or his son's mother think that he was attempting to drive a wedge between them. He knew Lexie would immediately accuse him of trying to gain permanent custody of Jake—something he wanted with all his heart even if he didn't have an aptitude for parenting. He could learn how to be a good parent, but he needed to have his son around in order to learn that. Antagonizing Lexie would definitely cause him to forfeit his custody rights.

"Maybe not." It was all Anderson would concede.

"Well, Jake clearly responds well to the attention that Marina's given him. Given that, wouldn't it make sense to have those two together even when he's not in school?"

Anderson frowned. Just where was Paige going with all this? "What are you suggesting? That I get Marina to adopt him?"

There were times that her brother was so thick, she could just scream. "Of course not."

"Then what?" he wanted to know impatiently.

"You're the big, smart brother," Paige reminded him, throwing his earlier self-description back at him. "You figure it out."

"Paige—" There was a warning note in Anderson's voice.

She could only lead him so far. After that, he was going to have to figure it out for himself. Otherwise, he'd accuse her of meddling and do the exact opposite of what she wanted to suggest with all her heart: that he go out with Marina and give them both a chance.

Paige pretended to look at her watch. "Oh, look at the time. Gotta go," she announced. With that, she got back behind the wheel of her vehicle. "Tell Jake I said hi—and think about what I said."

"Which part?" he wanted to know, exasperated.

"All of it," she told him just before she pulled away.

"No time," he called after her.

But the truth of it was, he did think about it. He thought about how he felt he was in over his head. Most of all, he thought about the petite redheaded teacher with the startling blue eyes. He was struggling to resist having anything to do with the woman, but he was really beginning to wonder if he wasn't allowing his own fear of any sort of involvement to get in the way of his son's welfare.

If what he'd seen at the town meeting and at Back to School Night were any indication, his son really did have a full-blown crush on his teacher. She could very well be the key to his being able to establish a decent relationship with Jake. At least it was worth a shot, he told himself.

He just hoped that he wasn't also shooting himself in the foot.

It was another half hour before Jerry Holder finally drove up in his beat-up pickup truck, bringing Jake with him.

"I brought my own hammer," Jake announced proudly as he bounced out of the passenger side of the truck. He held it up so that his father could see it for himself. Joining him, Jake looked back and forth along the long length of the fence. "Where do you want me to get started?"

"Why don't you work right alongside me?" Anderson suggested. He thought it best to keep an eye on the boy until he felt that Jake knew enough about the task to be allowed to work at his own pace.

Jake took another hard look at the long length of fencing. His small face puckered up a little.

"Are we fixing all of it?" he asked, sounding somewhat intimidated by the scope of the job.

Anderson looked at the fence, trying to see it through the young boy's eyes. He had to admit that from this angle, it looked as if it went on forever.

"Whatever needs fixing," he told his son.

"Oh." The single word was brimming with emotion. "Are we doing it all today?" he asked,

Anderson laughed. "No, not today. Today we're only going to do a little bit to get started." He pretended to look very solemn as he asked Jake, "That okay with you, cowboy?"

Jake bobbed his head up and down, clearly pleased at being consulted by his father this way. "It's okay with me," he said, and went to work.

Jake worked quietly alongside his father for close to twenty minutes before he finally and unexpectedly broke the silence.

His out-of-the-blue declaration was not exactly the kind that caused ripples of surprise to go undulating through the air.

"I really like Ms. Laramie," he told his father.

Jake looked so serious, it was hard for him not to laugh, but he managed to pull it off. "Really? I hadn't noticed."

"Well, I do," Jake solemnly confirmed. "I think that she's really nice." He paused then, his hammer dangling from his fingers as he seemed to ponder what he was about to say next. He began carefully, his eyes never leaving Anderson. "Dad?"

"Yes, Jake?" Anderson asked patiently. He'd decided that he was going to be open to anything his son had to say. This was brand-new territory that they were crossing and he didn't want to say anything that would have Jake closing up again.

Jake pressed his lips together as he searched for just the right words. "Do you think that maybe someday, we could invite Ms. Laramie and her daughter to the ranch for lunch or maybe dinner?" he asked.

"Maybe someday," Anderson echoed, knowing full well that it wasn't going to end there.

And it didn't.

"Someday soon?" Jake asked hopefully, rocking forward on his toes.

"Define *soon*," Anderson requested, appearing to continue to hammer down the next nail.

In reality, his mind was anywhere *but* on fixing the fence. He was bracing himself for what was coming—and for what he was going to have to say in order to make his son happy.

"I dunno," Jake answered. "Like maybe next week?"

"That soon?" Anderson knew he couldn't surrender immediately. It had to take at least a couple of seconds. "Jake, I don't know if—"

"Did you know that Sydney's never seen a horse?" Jake asked. "Not in her *whole* life," he stressed.

"Sydney?" Anderson questioned.

"Ms. Laramie's baby," Jake explained, his eyes never leaving his father.

Anderson remembered the expression on Marina's face when he surprised her by walking in on her when she was changing her daughter. He recalled the infant's little arms and legs waving in the air.

"Isn't Sydney about five months old?" he asked, taking a stab at the infant's age from her small size.

Again Jake nodded vigorously. "Yes, she is."

"At five months, she could have seen an elephant and I doubt if she would remember once she's a year old. At that age, nothing much registers," he assured his son, waiting to see what Jake came up with next.

He was surprised that his son didn't attempt to spin any yarns. Instead, he was very direct about the matter. "Then you're not going to invite them to the ranch?" Jake asked, looking crestfallen.

When the boy regarded him like that, Anderson knew that he would have moved heaven and earth to get him to smile again.

That was when Anderson resigned himself to losing this battle over Marina's invasion into his life. Jake had somehow, without a single shot being fired, won the war. His son had somehow managed to get the upper hand here by doing nothing more than being himself.

And, in order to make his son happy, he knew he was willing to do anything, even if it meant having to throw open his doors and invite that woman and her offspring into his home.

"On the contrary," he told Jake, "I am going to invite her to lunch."

Jake's eyes grew huge, brimming with happiness. "When?" he asked eagerly.

"When am I going to invite her, or when is she coming over?" Anderson asked, drawing the moment out.

"Both!" Jake cried.

He'd expected nothing else, Anderson thought. "I was thinking along the lines of inviting her to come to lunch next Saturday. That way it'll be light and Sydney can get to see the horses. Who knows, maybe she'll even get to ride one."

"But she's too little for that," Jake protested protectively.

He would have made a great big brother, Anderson thought. Too bad that wasn't going to happen. At least, not on his side, Anderson thought. Nonetheless, he was pleased to see these qualities in his son.

"Can you tell me when you're going to do it?" Jake asked hopefully. "When you're going to ask Ms. Laramie over?"

Anderson had no problem with that. "Sure, but why?" he asked, curious.

"That way, I can watch and listen. I won't even make a peep," Jake promised.

Then, in case there was any doubt, the boy crossed his heart making an elaborate show of sweeping his fingertips first in one direction and then in the other, forming a huge, albeit invisible, cross over his small heart.

Anderson suppressed a grin. "Okay, now

that that's settled, let's get back to work," he suggested.

"Let's!" Jake agreed, beaming as he grabbed up his hammer, looking ready and eager to follow his father anywhere.

Seeing him, Anderson knew he would have been willing to pay any price just to bask in that sort of gleeful approval.

Even if it meant spending the day with Jake's fifth-grade teacher.

Chapter 7

Out of the corner of his eye, Anderson could see his son in the family room.

Jake was hovering around instead of sitting on the sofa. He had the video controller in his hand, but unlike when he first arrived on the ranch, the boy wasn't playing. Despite the fact that there were lifelike characters flying back and forth across the TV screen, Jake wasn't even pretending to pay attention to them. Not since the boy had seen him pick up the receiver to make the call.

Anderson could see his son watching him in what he could only assume the boy believed to be a covert manner. Well, it looked like Jake could definitely rule out being a spy from his list of future careers, he thought, the corners of his mouth curving in amusement.

Every time he looked in Jake's direction, the boy would jerk his head down as if something about his controller had suddenly caught his complete, undivided attention.

But Anderson knew better. Jake was watching him. Watching and waiting for him to complete the phone call that would commit him to the fateful path he'd promised his son he would take—the path he didn't want to take. Inviting Marina Laramie and her daughter, Sydney, to come out to the ranch for the day.

C'mon, Dalton, how bad can it be? It's just for one afternoon out of your life. Before you know it, it'll be gone just like that—and you will have made your son one happy cowboy.

Anderson suppressed a sigh. The problem was he didn't want to call Marina. Didn't want to call her for a number of reasons. If he extended the invitation and Marina turned it down, Jake would be devastated and any good that had come from the association of teacher and student would have gone out the window. If, however, Marina *did* accept the invitation, then Jake would undoubtedly want her to come over again.

And again.

And again—until the woman would weave herself into the fabric of both their lives and there would be no escaping her. He knew that he really didn't want to go that route.

And then there were his sisters. Paige and Lani had turned into some sort of an annoying cheering section for the feisty little redheaded teacher, extolling Marina's virtues every time he wound up exchanging more than a couple of words with either of them.

If they caught wind of the fact that he'd actually invited Marina and Sydney to the house, that would be the end of peace as he knew it. He knew his sisters. They would immediately start planning their wedding no matter *what* he said to them about the invitation being extended to the woman strictly for Jake's sake and not his own.

Then there was that "other" reason. The one that entailed his complete reluctance to occupy the same general area as the vibrant fifth-grade teacher because—well, just because. She made him uneasy, made him remember that when it came to women, he didn't exactly have an outstanding track record. He didn't want to be attracted to a woman because attraction meant that the specter of disappointment and all that entailed would be waiting for him in the wings only a few steps away.

He'd much rather keep to himself than have to go through that. It was demoralizing.

Do it for Jake. This is for Jake, an insistent voice in his head whispered. The only reason he was even in this situation—having to call Marina's cell to tender the invitation—was because he was Jake's dad and it was up to him to extend the invitation since Jake couldn't very well do it on his own and be taken seriously. She was extroverted and properly unpredictable to a degree, but he sincerely doubted that Marina would just pop up on the porch and announce she was staying for lunch because Jake had invited her to do so.

He'd been psyching himself up now for fifteen minutes. Braced as he would ever be, Anderson brought the landline receiver to his ear.

Glancing one last time over his shoulder, he saw Jake watching his every move. At this point, the boy didn't even try to pretend to look away. Instead, with an encouraging grin, Jake gave him the thumbs-up sign.

His son was obviously hoping for the best. *That makes two of us, buddy.*

The only problem was, given this particular

scenario, Anderson didn't exactly know what "the best" outcome was in this case.

He looked down at the precise numbers that Jake had carefully written down on the piece of paper he'd handed him. The paper contained Marina's cell number, which Jake had gotten thanks to Paige.

He supposed that made sense, Anderson thought now, looking down at the phone number. After all, Paige and Marina were friends so of course his sister would have the other teacher's personal number. He had to shake off this feeling that it was all one giant conspiracy to pair him up with the teacher.

Taking another breath and feeling Jake's eyes all but boring into him, Anderson forced himself to complete the call. As it rang, he silently resigned himself to the inevitable.

But before he could complete his mental pep talk, Anderson heard the phone on the other end being picked up and someone on the other end saying, "Hello?"

The single word sounded like a self-contained symphony.

Anderson came very close to losing his nerve and just hanging up. And maybe he would have if he hadn't felt Jake's eyes all but glued to him the entire time. He couldn't disappoint the boy.

Here goes nothing.

"Hello, Ms. Laramie?"

"Yes?"

He could hear the slight quizzical note in her response. She didn't recognize his voice.

Last chance to bail, he thought, toying with the idea.

But if he bailed, he knew that he'd be disappointing Jake—and besides, bailing was the act of a coward. He knew that he was a lot of things, but a coward was not one of them.

Most especially when his son was watching him.

"Ms. Laramie, this is Anderson Dalton—Jake's father," he added almost awkwardly, as well as, he discovered, needlessly.

"I know who you are, Mr. Dalton," she assured him patiently. "Is there something that I can do for you?"

Transfer to another state before I do something we're both going to regret.

"Actually," he told her, "I'm calling about something that I could do for you."

She paused for a long moment before finally saying—rather stiffly at that, "I'm afraid you have me at a disadvantage."

That makes two of us, Anderson couldn't help thinking.

Belatedly he realized how Marina might have gotten the wrong idea from his response. Anderson cleared his throat, telling himself he needed to start over if this had a prayer of working out—for Jake, he tacked on again. This was all for Jake. He couldn't allow himself to lose sight of that.

"Let me start over," he began.

"Please," Marina urged.

He almost laughed at the unabashed earnestness of the request. He had a feeling she wouldn't have reacted well to his laughing at her and managed to refrain.

"Jake was telling me that Sydney's never ridden on a horse."

"No, she hasn't," Marina confirmed, sounding as if she wasn't sure if he was being serious. "You do realize that my daughter's only five months old."

"I figured she was around that age," Anderson admitted. He gave no indication that he knew perfectly well that a five-month-old did not belong on the back of a horse—at least not by herself. "But Jake seems really troubled that your daughter's gone all this time without having that experience."

He heard her laugh and he had to admit that there was something almost lyrically engaging about that sound. And he also had to admit that at least part of him was relieved that she didn't think he was either insensitive or crazy to even be talking about the idea of Sydney on horseback.

"You do have a very sensitive, thoughtful son, Mr. Dalton."

Marina smiled to herself as she thought of the boy. She had to bite back the urge to ask if Jake took after his mother. Anderson seemed more like the type to shoulder his way through the world—whether the world wanted to get out of the way or not.

"My 'very sensitive, thoughtful son' would like me to invite you and your daughter to come to the ranch for lunch and a little horseplay."

Marina stepped back into the land of confusion again. "Excuse me?"

"Jake wants Sydney to meet Fury."

That remark was even less clear than the first one. Was he deliberately trying to confuse her? Or was it her? "What?"

Anderson realized that the reference probably meant nothing to the woman, unless she was a trivia expert—or one of her students happened to be hooked on classic kids' TV shows.

"Jake named the horse I gave him after this old, old TV show he saw on one of those kids' channels." And then, just in case she was worried that the name fit the horse, he reassured her. "Trust me, Fury doesn't live up to her name. The horse makes molasses look like it's moving fast. Jake is a city boy—he likes to make things sound dangerous. But I knew he had to take it slow when it came to riding and Fury is really even gentler than an old gray mare."

"If you say so," she replied, not totally convinced that he was telling her the truth.

But the one thing she was convinced of was that Anderson loved his son. Anyone who was around the two of them for more than a couple of minutes could see that was the case.

She heard what sounded like Anderson clearing his throat. The next moment, he started to speak. "Well, anyway, Jake wanted me to invite the two of you to the ranch whenever it was convenient for you to come out."

Marina noticed how he emphasized the fact that the invitation was coming from his son. If she was reading correctly between the lines, that meant that he was extending the invitation under protest.

"Tell Jake that I think it's very sweet of him to invite us, but I'm afraid Sydney and I will have to take a rain check."

"Oh. Sure. Okay." Anderson would have thought that he'd be relieved. After all, that was what he wanted, wasn't it? To have her turn down his invitation. And he *was* relieved—to some extent.

But he was also experiencing something else. Something, for lack of a better description, that felt akin to disappointment.

It was official. He was going crazy, he thought.

And then, to cinch his impression, he heard himself asking her, "Mind if I ask why?"

Marina had expected Anderson to accept her declination—maybe even cheer a little—and just hang up. He certainly hadn't sounded as if he was eager for her to accept the invitation.

So why was he asking her to give him a reason?

He knew the answer to her declination as well as she did.

"Look, Mr. Dalton, I wouldn't want to put you out," she told him.

"Put me out?" he repeated, completely perplexed. What was she talking about? More than anything, he wished that women would come with some sort of an instruction booklet. It would make life a hell of a lot easier. "What makes you think having you come out to the ranch would be 'putting me out'?"

She sighed. She was beginning to think that the man took a certain perverse pleasure in making things difficult.

"I'm trying to be accommodating here, Mr. Dalton," she began and got no further.

"I don't understand," Anderson said. "If you were trying to be accommodating, wouldn't you have said yes to the invitation?"

"To your *son's* invitation," she emphasized. Didn't he see the difference?

He missed the point for a minute and was about to tell her again that he didn't understand what she was trying to tell him when he managed to successfully play back her words in his mind.

"Wait, what? Why did you just refer to it as Jake's invitation?" he wanted to know.

"Well, isn't it?"

He saw no reason to lie. After all, this had started out specifically because it *was* Jake's idea. "Yes."

The word felt like a burst of cold water, shocking her in its honesty. Well, at least he wasn't trying to snow her, she told herself.

Then again, he didn't seem to care about her feelings, either. It would have been nice to have him indulge in even a little white lie.

She discovered that she was having trouble holding on to her temper. That only happened when she had exhausted her own deep well of patience.

"Anyway," she managed to say, "the only thing that should matter to you is that I'm letting you off the hook."

"You keep talking about some 'hook.' I'm not *on* a hook," he insisted, shortly.

"Yes, you are," she countered, digging in. She absolutely hated being lied to. The worst truth was better than the best lie in her opinion. "Jake asked you to invite us and you did, but it's obvious that the invitation to come to the ranch is coming from him and not from you."

The woman was coming close to dancing on his last nerve. "It might be obvious to you, but not to me."

"Don't try to spare my feelings, Mr. Dalton," she cautioned. "It's a little too late for that."

He was about to let it go at that, thinking it was for the best for both of them since he firmly believed that the woman could make a saint crazy. But then he caught sight of Jake watching him, looking so hopeful that it all but stabbed him right through his heart. Because of that, he gave it one more try.

For Jake.

"The invitation is really from both of us," he informed her. Then, before she had a chance to launch into some sort of full-scale rebuttal, he shot down any possible argument she had in her arsenal.

"Do you really think I'd be inviting you to come to the ranch for the day if I didn't want you and your daughter here?"

Okay, so it was a lie, he silently admitted, but it was a well-intentioned one and it had been undertaken for the best of reasons. Namely because something about Marina Laramie not only made his son happy, but made him light up like the proverbial Christmas tree.

He would have extended an invitation to a Tasmanian she-devil if the prospect of having one over to the ranch would have had the same effect on Jake.

He realized that the other end of the line had gone quiet and for a second, Anderson thought he'd lost her because she'd seen through his fabrication—otherwise known as a lie—and hung up. He hoped not because that meant that he would have to call her back.

"Are you still there?" he asked, raising his voice.

"Yes, I'm still here," he heard her say in a voice that was definitely subdued.

He plowed on. "So what's your answer?"

"You're really asking us to the ranch?" she asked, wanting to make sure one final time.

"I could try to get it across with hand puppets," he volunteered. "But you really wouldn't be able to see that over the phone—I'm calling from a landline," he explained, vaguely aware that these days, there were ways for people calling one another on the phone to be able to see the other person.

Personally, he thought that the whole world needed to take a few steps back and have a time-out. There was just too much tech stuff out there for his liking. It interfered with human relationships—when there were any, he quickly inserted, mentally backing away from the subject.

"So, what's it going to be?" he asked her. "What do I tell Jake—and what are you going to tell me?" he added out of the blue.

It was almost as if the words had just come out on their own volition without any prompting or effort on his part.

"What day would you like us over?" she

asked him tentatively. What was she doing? She felt as if she was about to make a fifteen-foot dive into a half-filled teacup. Her stomach clenched, even as excitement skittered over her nerve endings.

An inexplicable feeling of triumph volleyed through Anderson. He didn't attempt to analyze it, understand it or even question why it suddenly turned up. Those were all things he told himself he'd deal with later. Right now he needed to nail down the woman's response to the invitation before she changed her mind or had second, paralyzing thoughts. If she did, Jake would be severely disappointed. It was his job to make sure that didn't happen.

That was his story and he was sticking to it.

"So is that a yes?" he asked her.

"It's a yes," she agreed.

"How does tomorrow sound?" he asked. "I know it's kind of last-minute, but it's a Sunday so I thought you both might be free."

"As it so happens," she told him in carefully measured out words, "we are both free. Tomorrow sounds fine."

"Great. Why don't you and your daughter plan on coming out here around nine and we'll make a day of it." He gave her the straightforward directions, ending with, "You can't miss it."

She laughed softly. "I wouldn't take any bets on that if I were you." Then, before he could interject anything else, she said, "We'll see you there at nine," and with that, she hung up.

Chapter 8

Marina's sigh seemed to echo all around. Why was she doing this to herself? Sunday was supposed to be a day of rest, not a day of extreme tension.

She shouldn't have said yes.

"This is a mistake." She looked down at her daughter. "Listen very carefully, Sydney, because Mommy's not going to say these words very often during your formative years, at least not about herself where you can hear them. I think I've made a mistake saying yes to Jake's daddy. A really big mistake."

Marina had stopped her futile search within the bedroom of her small apartment. There was no point in looking for the right outfit to wear, she thought, feeling more and more insecure by the minute.

In an effort to calm down, she'd begun talking to her daughter as if she were an equal and a confidant instead of an infant strapped into her car seat on the floor.

For her part, Sydney was following her around the room with her eyes, looking as if she was hanging on every word even as she was trying to shove her tiny fist into her mouth and swallow it whole.

"I know that every woman is supposed to say this sometime in her lifetime," she told Sydney, "but in my case, it's true. I don't have anything to wear."

She'd gone through all her clothes and nothing looked right to her. She was attempting to find something casual, but all she could find were outfits that were either too formal, or looked as if she'd spent the morning scrubbing floors—and gotten the worst of it.

"I know, I know," Marina continued with her conversation, filling in what she felt would have been Sydney's responses if her daughter was capable of making responses. "You want to see the horsies but we can do that some other time—with somebody else's daddy doing the hosting, not Jake's daddy."

Sinking down on the edge of her bed she looked down at her daughter in earnest and for the second time in as many minutes, she sighed.

"You're right, we're not exactly awash in social invitations, are we? But they'll come. Just you wait, they'll come." Sydney made a gurgling sound. Marina blew out a breath, resigned. "But you want to go now, don't you? Okay, Mommy will just have to put her brave smile on and face this like an adult. After all, if I can deal with a roomful of eleven-year-olds, I can certainly deal with one adult. It's not like he's going to bite me or anything, right?"

Sydney gurgled again and this time, bobbed her head a little, which Marina took to be a nod. She got up again. "Good talk, Sydney. Good talk."

Just then, the doorbell rang and Marina could feel everything inside her instantly freezing up. Every insecurity she'd previously experienced was back, bringing along a friend.

"Maybe it's not too late to make a getaway out the back window," she said aloud, glancing toward it longingly. The doorbell rang again and Marina sighed. "Too late." Looking down at the outfit she'd wound up in—worn jeans and a blue-gray pullover—she shook her head. There was absolutely no time to change again. "This is going to have to do."

Sydney jabbered, as if responding to that statement.

"Right, easy for you to say," Marina told her. "You look adorable in everything."

She picked up the car seat and carried her daughter into her living room. Once there, she parked Sydney on the floor beside the sofa.

"Coming," she called out when the doorbell rang a third time.

Opening the door, Marina found herself looking up at Anderson Dalton. For some reason, he looked taller today than he had the other times.

A *lot* taller.

Or maybe that was just her nerves making him *look* taller.

But he smelled nice, she couldn't help noticing. He smelled of sunshine and wind.

Marina felt her stomach tightening and prayed that this outing she'd agreed to wasn't going to be something she was going to regret.

"Sorry it took me so long to get to the door," she apologized. "I was in the bedroom, looking for something to wear."

His eyes skimmed over her slowly—as if appraising what she had on, she couldn't help thinking. "I see you found it," he murmured.

The sound of his voice made the ripples in her stomach increase to storm-warning size. She shifted her eyes to Anderson's shadow, who had moved right to his father's side the moment he heard her voice.

On familiar ground again, Marina grinned at him. "Hi, Jake."

The boy's chest seemed to immediately puff up in response to her greeting. "Hi!"

Only when her eyes shifted back to him, Anderson realized he was staring at her. Marina had divided her hair into two pigtails and looked like a kid herself instead of the mother of one and the teacher of many. He mumbled a greeting, realizing that he hadn't done so when she came to the door. And then he felt compelled to explain.

"When you didn't answer the door after I rang the doorbell two times, I was going to leave," Anderson confessed. "I didn't think you were home, but Jake didn't want to give up so fast. He made me ring again."

"I call that patient stubbornness," Marina told him, smiling fondly at the boy. "It's a very good quality to have." She turned her attention back to Anderson. "That means he doesn't give up right away when things don't go his way."

"Oh, he can be pretty stubborn, all right," Anderson vouched, thinking of how persistent Jake had been until he'd gotten him to invite his teacher over against his own best instincts.

Looking past Marina into the living room, Anderson saw the swinging arms and legs first, then realized that he was looking at Marina's daughter, who, if she hadn't been strapped into the car seat, appeared ready for takeoff like a tiny helicopter.

"You need any help with that?" he asked, nodding at the baby. "You know, carrying it?"

What *was* it about this woman that turned him into an awkward, tongue-tripping idiot? He was behaving like the people he held in low esteem or actual contempt most of the time.

"The car seat," Anderson specified as an afterthought.

"I know what you meant," Marina assured him. "And no, I don't. Carrying around this much weight has become second nature to me. I don't even know I'm doing it. And," she added, "truthfully, lugging the car seat around has helped me build up my biceps."

But Anderson had already moved past her

and was picking up the car seat with Sydney in it before she had a chance to get to her daughter.

"I've got it," he told her matter-of-factly, as if this was business as usual instead of an outing he would have preferred to have no part of.

"What's a biceps?" Jake wanted to know, practically skipping next to her as they went outside and toward the truck.

The cab of Anderson's truck was large enough to accommodate all of them, including Sydney's car seat. Anderson had checked all that out beforehand. Otherwise, he would have been forced to borrow his sister Lindsay's car for the errand—and that would have required way too much explaining.

Following Anderson to his vehicle, Marina paused for a moment to answer the boy's question. "Make a muscle," she instructed. When he did, she pointed to the tiny ridge that was formed. "There," she told him, "that's your biceps."

Jake turned his head and looked at his upper arm as if seeing it for the first time. "I have one."

Marina never hesitated. "Absolutely. And it'll get to be very big if you do your exercises," she assured him and then added encouragingly, "It looks like you've already gotten started."

Jake beamed in response. "Maybe a little," he confided.

"Well, it's very impressive. Keep it up." Marina turned her attention to Anderson's struggles with her daughter's car seat. "Here, let me." Very gently, she edged him out of the way. "It's very frustrating until you get the hang of it," she said matter-of-factly.

Within a few seconds, she'd untangled the hook Anderson had gotten caught in the back of the seat and successfully attached Sydney's car seat to the truck's seat.

"There," Marina declared with relief. "Done."

He took her word for it. It certainly looked as if it was well secured. "I guess maybe I could use some of the patient stubbornness you were talking about," Anderson observed.

Getting into the backseat next to her daughter, Marina buckled herself in.

"I thought that was where Jake got it from," she said innocently. "You."

Her answer struck him as funny. "Not hardly." Anderson laughed shortly. "He probably developed it trying to impress you."

She was about to deny having anything to do with it when Jake climbed into the backseat next to her. She looked at her student in surprise.

"Don't you want to sit up front next to your dad, Jake?" She didn't want the boy hurting his father's feelings by having so blatantly picked her over him. "Most boys want to be right up front, where the action is."

But Jake, she quickly found out, wasn't like most boys.

"No, that's okay, Ms. Laramie. I'd rather be back here with you."

Marina leaned over and whispered to the boy, "You don't want to hurt your dad's feelings, do you? He'll think you don't like him if you sit back here with me instead of up front with him."

Anderson watched the little exchange in his rearview mirror. Since Marina was whispering to his son, he didn't hear what was being said, but he felt he could make a pretty educated guess.

"That's okay," he assured Marina as well as his son. "I don't mind him sitting back there with you if he wants. Jake is just trying to make you feel more welcome."

Marina wasn't sure if that was actually true or not, but she grasped at the excuse that Anderson had handed her and gave the boy a quick one-armed hug.

"Well, he certainly accomplished that," she told Jake fondly.

Jake's eyes sparkled. "We've got a surprise for you," he confided in what amounted to a stage whisper. "You and Sydney."

"A surprise? I love surprises," she told him with the proper enthusiasm, knowing that was what Jake was hoping for. "I can't wait."

She couldn't have said anything better to Jake if she had tried, Anderson thought, catching sight of his son's face in his rearview mirror.

His son looked proud enough to burst and seemed as if he could hardly contain himself. Jake gave the distinct impression that any second now, he'd go off like a Roman candle.

She had a hell of a great effect on his son, Anderson thought. Maybe having this woman here for the afternoon might turn out to be a good thing after all.

He realized that he could probably stand to learn a few things from her—whether he liked the idea of not.

"Do you want a hint?" Jake was asking, fidgeting in his seat and moving his feet back and forth, like someone who was desperately in need of channeling his energy somewhere.

"Well, I'm pretty good at picking up hints," Marina told her student, urging him on because she sensed that Jake wanted her to. "It won't spoil the surprise, will it?"

Damn, but she was good, Anderson couldn't help thinking. She really looked as if she was having a serious conversation with his son rather than the kind most adults had with children—a few words before they were brushed off.

Moreover, he could tell that Jake was totally eating all this up.

This woman was really worth observing more closely, Anderson told himself. He was rather certain that he could pick up a few pointers from her on how to communicate with his son. With all his heart, he really did want to build a better, closer relationship with Jake. That was, after all, he reminded himself, the reason he'd given in and invited Marina over in the first place.

Glancing up, Marina's eyes met Anderson's in the rearview mirror. For the last few minutes she'd thought she felt his eyes on her and she looked up, thinking perhaps she was just imagining things.

But she wasn't.

Anderson seemed to be watching her like a hawk. Why? Did he expect her to do something to upset his son? The man hadn't struck her as the protective type, but he obviously was. Marina viewed that as a good thing, even though it made her feel as if she was under a microscope. But she would gladly put up with it, for Jake's sake, given this rather delicate situation he found himself in.

"Jake," Anderson cautioned, "why don't you hold off on the hints? I'm sure Ms. Laramie likes to be surprised and she already said that she's very good at unraveling clues. You don't want to spoil her surprise for her, now do you?"

"Uh-uh," Jake piped up, shaking his head from side to side so hard that his straight light brown hair swung back and forth.

"I guess that I'll just have to wait," Marina said stoically, playing along.

"It'll be worth it," Jake assured her, his excitement once again bubbling up to the surface. "You'll like it." He glanced toward her daughter. "So will Sydney." The little girl made a sound in response to her name and Jake declared happily, "Did you hear her, Ms. Laramie? She agrees with me."

"Certainly sounds that way to me," Marina replied, doing, Anderson thought, a more than credible job of keeping a straight face.

She raised her eyes to meet Anderson's

again, hoping that there would be something there to give her a clue as to whether she should be braced for something, or if his son was getting excited just because he had gotten caught up in the visit and the promise of the day that was ahead of them.

From the way she saw Anderson's eyes crinkle as he looked at her, she realized that the man had to be smiling.

It was going to be all right, she silently promised herself. Whatever the surprise was, she felt fairly confident that there wasn't going to be something overwhelming going on. She began to relax and lower her guard.

And then it hit her.

The tension she'd felt ever since she'd agreed to this outing and had hung up the phone yesterday was gone. She was actually relaxed and, in a way, even looking forward to spending the day with her daughter on the ranch. She genuinely liked Jake and wanted to be able to help the boy fit into a home-life setting, something that she felt he both needed and deserved.

As for Anderson, he seemed somewhat abrupt at times, but she could tell that he loved his son and, bottom line, that was all that counted.

She rather envied Jake that. He had something that her daughter had been deprived of—a father who cared.

"Dad and I made lunch for you," Jake announced out of the blue. "We did it ahead of time," he added proudly. "Well, Dad made it and I helped."

Now *that* surprised her. "Your dad cooks?"

The tone of her voice had Anderson raising his eyes and looking at her in the mirror again. "Does that surprise you?"

She hadn't meant to say that out loud. Caught, she had to confess. "No disrespect intended but—yes."

"The best chefs in the world are men," Anderson pointed out.

"A handful," Marina allowed. "But that doesn't change the fact that a lot of men aren't sure how to even boil water."

Ordinarily, he would have just disregarded her comment, letting it pass and not caring one way or the other what she believed or thought. But for some reason, he didn't want her having that kind of a negative image of him.

"In my family," Anderson heard himself saying as they neared the ranch, "everyone was taught to pull their own weight and at least knows how to cook well enough to survive."

"Then I'll look forward to lunch," Marina

assured him, allowing just a glimmer of her amusement to show through.

"We've got milk for Sydney," Jake piped up, not to be left out, "'cause Dad said that she can't chew her food like I can."

"She can't," Marina confirmed, then explained, "because she only has three teeth."

Jake looked at her, concerned. "The janitor in my old elementary school, Mr. Wilson, he didn't have any of his teeth and he said he lost 'em in a fighting match."

"A boxing match?" Marina supplied, trying to get the details of his story straight.

Jake nodded. "Yeah, that's it, a boxing match. You saw it?" he asked. It was obvious that he thought since she was familiar with the term, that meant that she had to have been there to witness the event.

"No," she told him. "Just a lucky guess."

Jake cocked his head, studying her in fascination. "Are you lucky?"

Was she?

Unbidden, her eyes glanced up and lit on Anderson's in the rearview mirror. Out of nowhere the words slipped out. "At times."

Chapter 9

"This is all yours?" Marina asked in a voice that was just a little above a hushed whisper.

She had been growing progressively more awestruck as the miles had gone by. The land they'd been traveling on to get here was nothing short of overwhelmingly impressive. Squinting just a little, Marina thought she could make out a corral in the distance. There looked to be several horses milling about within its confines.

"Mine and the family's," Anderson told her as he drove. "I run the place for them but the ranch actually belongs to my father, Ben. Ranching really doesn't interest him all that much and his law firm keeps him pretty busy most of the time." Anderson shrugged good-naturedly. "I have no head for the law, but I like working with my hands, so this arrangement works out to everyone's advantage."

Pulling his truck up in front of the house, Anderson turned off the engine, got out and then opened the rear passenger door for his guests.

"Well, this is it."

Marina peered out through the window before beginning to remove the straps from around Sydney's car seat. He had pulled up before a one story ranch house with simple, strong lines. It suited Anderson, she thought.

As she began undoing the vehicle's restraining straps, she saw that Jake, after unbuckling himself, was doing the same on his side of the car seat.

"That's all right, Jake," Marina told him. "I can do that."

But the boy continued, pausing only to look up and tell her, "I like helping."

She couldn't very well argue with that. She knew it was a trait to encourage.

"Well, that's lucky, because I like being helped," she responded. "And I very much appreciate yours."

The remark only managed to spur Jake on and he worked quicker.

"Done!" Jake announced, raising his hands up in the air like a rodeo cowboy when he had managed to successfully finish roping a calf.

"Me, too," Marina said, matching his tone. She edged out of the truck, wanting to be on firm ground before easing her daughter out.

But she had no sooner gotten out of the truck than Anderson was moving her over, out of the way.

"Okay," he told her. "I'll take it from here."

Before she could demur or offer any protest, Anderson was taking both car seat and baby out of the back of his truck. Then he ushered her toward the house, still holding on to the car seat.

"Let's go inside," Anderson said. It sounded more like a command than a suggestion. "Jake said he wanted to show you around. I didn't think you'd mind," he said, giving her a way out if she wanted it.

"Well, then, let's get to it," Marina urged cheerfully, placing one arm lightly around the boy's shoulders.

His son, Anderson noted, was now beaming so hard, he had a feeling that if the power in

Rust Creek Falls went out, the boy could light the whole town up.

Anderson caught himself smiling as he led the way into the house.

The tour of the ranch house went rather quickly, with Jake doing virtually all of the narrating as they passed from one room to another. Anderson was surprised that his son had actually picked up so much information about the place in the last three months. If anyone had asked him, he would have sworn that Jake was oblivious to everything that was going on around him, focusing exclusively on the small world that existed within the video games he seemed to be so attached to.

Live and learn, Anderson thought, happy that he had turned out to be wrong about Jake.

At the end of the impromptu tour, they ended up in the kitchen.

"And here we are, back in the kitchen," Jake declared just before he quietly slipped away, after giving his father a wink.

Marina shifted her daughter to her other hip and drew closer to her official host.

"Where's he going?" she asked, surprised that the boy had decided to disappear.

"Well, a couple of weeks ago, I would have

said that he's gone to his room to play a video game, but since he seemed so caught up in showing you the lay of the land, I'd say he's gone to fetch the surprise that he got for you."

Marina looked at him quizzically. "I don't think I understand."

"You will," was all that Anderson was willing to tell her.

Did he want her to prod him? "You're being very mysterious."

Anderson didn't debate the matter one way or another. Instead, he just told her, "Jake would be very disappointed if I spoiled his surprise."

That still didn't really address her concerns. So she came right out and asked, "Should I be braced for something?"

Anderson laughed then. It was a genuine laugh, tinged with amusement. The sound seemed to embrace her. Any concerns she might have had began to melt away.

"Lady," he told her, "you strike me as someone who's already braced for anything that might come her way."

She wasn't sure if he was giving her a compliment, but she liked to think that he was.

Jake chose that moment to come back into the room. He had a bag with him from one of the local stores in town and he held it out to her.

"This is for Sydney," Jake told her proudly. "She can't open it, so you have to."

Touched, Marina accepted it, then held up the bag for her daughter to see.

"Jake got you a present, Sydney," Marina told the baby, shifting the tiny girl again so that she could open the bag.

"Dad paid for it," Jake told her, wanting her to have all the details. "But I picked it out."

Marina glanced at the quiet man at her side. "You have an incredibly honest son, Mr. Dalton. Anyone else would have taken all the credit himself," she concluded, looking at Jake. She smiled her approval at the boy.

The latter beamed in response. "Open it, open it," he urged her excitedly.

Marina did as he asked. Reaching into the bag, she took her daughter's gift out.

"It's a cowboy hat," she cried. "A really sweet, tiny cowboy hat." She was delighted with it. "Look, Sydney," she said, holding it up in front of her daughter. "Your very first cowboy hat."

"Here, let me help," Anderson volunteered, taking the hat from Marina and gently slipping it onto the infant's head.

Once it was on, he tightened the drawstrings beneath her small chin just enough to keep the hat from slipping off her head.

"She looks like a real cowgirl!" Jake enthused, visibly happy that he'd been part of the "transformation" process.

Sydney kept turning her head, as if trying to catch sight of what it was atop her head. After several tries, she finally gave up.

Jake suddenly turned toward his father. "Can we take them out to the corral?" he wanted to know, eager to start the next phase of his plan.

"Maybe Ms. Laramie would like something to eat or drink first before we go outside again," Anderson suggested.

But Marina shook her head. "No, we're fine and I'm sure that Sydney would love to see your horses," she told Jake. "I know I would," she admitted.

"Okay, let's go back out to the truck," Anderson said, beginning to lead the way to the front door.

"Why the truck?" Marina wanted to know, surprised and a little disappointed. "Have you changed your mind about going to the corral and decided to take us home?"

He looked at her quizzically, wondering where she could have gotten that idea. "No,

I'm taking the truck so that I can drive you over to the corral," Anderson explained.

"Can't we just walk?"

"Well, sure we can," Anderson agreed. "But I thought that walking all that way over to the corral might be too far for you and the baby."

Just what sort of women was this man used to? Marina couldn't help wondering. Granted, she wasn't exactly pioneer stock, but she didn't fall apart at the mention of a brisk walk, either.

"Sydney and I really aren't that fragile, Mr. Dalton. And walking is a very good form of exercise," she added, glancing at Jake in order to include the boy in this, as well. "I don't get a chance to do it often enough," she confided to Anderson.

Jake looked up at his father. "Can we, Dad? Can we walk there?"

Anderson wasn't about to be the villain of the piece. He'd only made the offer for Marina's benefit. If she wanted to walk, then that was fine with him.

"Lead the way, Jake," Anderson told his son. As Jake took off like a flash, Anderson called after him, "Walk, Jake, don't run."

Jake came to almost a skidding halt, his face flushing slightly as he turned around to look at his teacher.

"Sorry. I forgot. You can't run."

"Who says I can't run?" Marina wanted to know. "I just can't run when I'm holding the baby."

"'Cause you don't want to drop her?" Jake earnestly asked.

"That would be a good reason, yes," Marina agreed, doing her best to suppress the laughter that was bubbling up in her throat, threatening to spill out.

"I can take her from you if you feel like stretching your legs," Anderson volunteered. His offer took her completely by surprise.

Marina was about to thank him, but tell Anderson that it was all right, that she would carry her daughter. It wasn't that she didn't trust him, it was just that she didn't know how familiar he was with what it took to walk that distance while carrying an infant—a possibly wiggling infant—in his arms.

But the next moment, she decided to keep the words to herself when she looked at his face. There was something there that allayed her fears about turning her infant daughter over to this man.

So instead, Marina told him, "That would be very nice of you," as she handed her daughter over, placing Sydney into Anderson's arms.

She watched, fascinated, as Anderson's face instantly softened right in front of her eyes. Then and there he seemed to bond with her daughter in a way she would have never expected.

The next second, Jake was declaring, "Race you!" The announcement snapped Marina out of her self-imposed trance.

"You're on," Marina responded and then quickly began to run toward the corral.

Marina was careful to keep up, but to never outpace her student, who gleefully made a beeline for the corral, which was the intended finish line.

They reached it almost at the same time, together, with Jake getting to the corral just a few feet ahead of her.

"I won!" he laughed gleefully.

Marina sagged slightly against the corral, even as she affectionately ruffled his hair. "You sure did," she agreed.

"But you ran good," Jake was quick to add, not wanting to hurt her feelings.

"I ran 'well,'" Marina told him, correcting his grammar.

Caught up in the moment and the win, the correction flew right over Jake's head.

"That, too," Jake said, nodding his head. It

caused her to laugh, charmed by his innocent intensity.

"Let's catch our breath while we wait for your dad," she suggested, pointing in the distance to the man and her baby.

Anderson raised his hand in a wave.

As he watched Marina, he couldn't help thinking she didn't run like a stereotypical girl. From his vantage point, she ran like a sleek thoroughbred.

Marina Laramie was a thing of beauty to observe, he couldn't help noting.

Sydney made a noise and he glanced down at the infant he was carrying in his arms.

"You a mind reader, hot stuff?" he asked, amused, pretending that the infant's noise was a commentary on what he'd been thinking. "It was just an observation. I didn't mean anything by it."

In response, Sydney made what sounded suspiciously like a cooing noise.

The sound warmed Anderson and made him sad at the same time. He'd missed experiencing these sorts of small moments with his own son. Missed so much in those ten years that he'd been kept in the dark about Jake's existence. He couldn't find it in his heart to forgive Lexie for that.

He liked to think that he would have made a decent father, if these feelings that he was now experiencing were any sort of indication of what fatherhood would have been like.

"I won!" Jake called out to him gleefully as he approached with Marina's daughter. "Did you see me, Dad? I won!"

"You certainly did," Marina confirmed with a smile. Turning toward Anderson, she held out her arms. "Give her to me. She's got to be getting heavy for you."

But Anderson deliberately ignored her request. "Catch your breath first," he told Marina. "This little charmer isn't heavy at all. I think I can manage holding your daughter for a little while longer."

As a matter of fact, he thought, though he kept it to himself, he rather enjoyed it.

"She does look cute like that," Marina commented, referring to the pint-size cowboy hat atop her daughter's head.

"Can I show Ms. Laramie the big surprise now?" Jake asked excitedly, dancing from foot to foot as he looked at his father.

"Doesn't that boy ever tire out?" Marina asked, marveling at his energy.

"Not to my knowledge. Okay, Jake, bring over the surprise," he told his son. As the boy

ducked into the corral and ran off to the stable
just beyond, Anderson turned so that he was
facing Marina. He didn't want his son to hear.
"You let him win."

Marina looked up at him, an innocent expression on her face. "No, I didn't."

"I'm not much of an expert when it comes
to a lot of things," he told her. "But you were
definitely holding back. No point in denying
it, Ms. Laramie. I know what I know."

"Marina," she corrected him.

He looked at her, confused for a moment.
And then he realized what she was saying.
"Tell you what, you stop calling me Mr. Dalton
and I'll stop calling you Ms. Laramie. Deal?"

"Deal," she said, eyeing Sydney. "As long
as you give me back my daughter."

"You drive a hard bargain, Marina," he told
her, amused. With that, he handed back the
infant.

Just in time for Jake to return and bring over
his big surprise.

The surprise was trotting right behind him
on four very sturdy hooves.

Chapter 10

Jake's surprise turned out to be a beautiful, chestnut-colored mare.

"This is Fury," he proudly told his teacher. "She's my horse and she's going to give Sydney her very first horseback ride."

Marina knew that the boy meant well, but there was no way she was about to allow Sydney to get on the back of that horse.

She hugged her daughter a little closer as she looked over her shoulder at her host. What was Jake's father thinking? she silently demanded.

As if reading her mind, Anderson told her, "Don't let the name fool you. They don't come any gentler than Lady Fury, here." Leaning over the corral fence, he patted the mare's muzzle.

Maybe the horse was gentle, but the mare was also very big—and Sydney was very little. "Be that as it may—" Marina began only to have Anderson interrupt her as if she hadn't said anything.

"Since Jake seemed to think it was so important for Sydney to experience her very first horseback ride, I thought that I could hold her in my arms while I rode around the inside of the corral on Fury."

She supposed that was a way to appease the boy and yet keep Sydney safe.

Marina looked at the mare, still a little skeptical about the idea. "And you're sure that she's gentle?"

"No question about it," Anderson assured her. "I give you my word."

"Absolutely!" Jake chimed in enthusiastically. "Dad wouldn't let me ride on any other horse to start with. Fury's so gentle, she's almost poky," the boy told her solemnly.

She didn't want to come across as being overprotective—and they were both doing their best to accommodate Sydney.

"I guess that's good enough for me," Marina

told them. She turned toward Anderson. "Hold Sydney while I get on the horse."

That wasn't what he'd just proposed. "You?" Anderson asked.

"Me." She saw the doubtful look in Anderson's eyes as he took the baby. "I can ride a horse. Don't look so surprised. After all, this *is* Montana. What kind of a Montanan would I be if I didn't know how to ride?" Holding on to the saddle horn, Marina swung into the saddle, then held her arms out for her daughter. "The baby, please," she prompted when Anderson made no attempt to hand over Sydney to her.

After what seemed like a long moment, Anderson surrendered the baby. "I wasn't going to drop her," he protested, thinking that might have been the reason Marina didn't want him to take the baby for a ride.

"I know. I wasn't insinuating that you were. I just wanted to be the one to give Sydney her first horseback ride," Marina told him.

"I can lead my horse around the corral for you," Jake volunteered enthusiastically, his eyes shining with excitement.

Marina was about to tell her student that she wanted to just circle the corral herself, but she saw the eagerness in his eyes and couldn't find it in her heart to refuse Jake.

So she didn't.

"I'd be honored if you led Fury around the corral for Sydney and me," she told the boy.

Jake beamed so hard, she thought his face was seriously in danger of cracking. And then he suddenly turned solemn, as if he was about to take on a huge responsibility.

"I won't go too fast," Jake promised.

"I have every faith in you," Marina told the boy as he began to lead Fury around the perimeter of the corral by her bit.

True to his word, Jake led the mare around slowly—almost too slowly.

As they passed by Anderson, who was perched on the top rung of the corral, she noticed the amusement on his face.

"Gentle enough for you, Marina?" he asked.

"The point is that she's gentle enough for Sydney," Marina responded. "And she is."

Anderson inclined his head. "That's all that matters," he agreed.

She glanced down at her daughter, who was cooing with delight. Jake seemed to take credit for her enjoyment, and Marina had a feeling that he would have gone on indefinitely if she'd let him. She let Jake enjoy himself for as long as she thought prudent, and then she whistled.

When he looked at her over his shoulder,

she told him, "I think that maybe Sydney's had enough for her first time, Jake. She's getting tired." The little girl had grown quiet and looked as if she'd fall asleep.

Jake reluctantly nodded his head. "Okay."

He led Fury back over to where his father was still sitting on the fence.

"Had enough?" Anderson asked the taller of Fury's two passengers.

"Sydney has. I could go on riding," Marina confided. "It's been a long time since I've had a chance to go out riding."

"Maybe we can do something about that," Anderson said casually as he took the sleepy infant from Marina.

It sounded as if he was extending an invitation for a return visit, Marina thought, then told herself that she was reading things into his comment. He was probably just being kind, nothing more.

It really had been a long time since she'd gotten out, Marina thought. Maybe that was why she was guilty of being a little too eager and of reading things into Anderson's casual conversation.

They went back to the house and this time, they had lunch. Anderson had prepared hamburger patties ahead of time.

"It's our secret recipe," Jake confided to her as his father placed several patties on an indoor grill. Within a few minutes, the air was filled with a mouthwatering, tempting aroma.

"That smells delicious," Marina told her host, realizing how hungry she was. She'd been too nervous to have any breakfast this morning, she recalled.

"That's the general idea," Anderson replied, taking her comment in stride. "Two burgers enough for you?"

"Oh, more than enough," Marina assured him. "I get filled up quickly."

Anderson laughed, glancing at his son. "That's not our problem, is it, Jake?"

The boy grinned from ear to ear, eyeing the burgers' progress. "Nope."

"For a skinny kid," Anderson told her, "Jake's a regular bottomless pit."

Marina glanced at the boy. He was thin and wiry, without an ounce of fat on him.

"A lot of people would kill to be like that," she told both Anderson and Jake.

Her host looked to have everything under control. Still, she wanted to pitch in. "Is there anything I can do?" she wanted to know.

"You can eat," Anderson told her as he flipped the first batch of hamburgers onto a plate. He set the plate down on the table, putting it next to the buns and a platter of sliced tomatoes and lettuce, and a few condiments.

"Besides that," she countered.

Anderson shook his head. "Can't think of a thing," he answered. He arranged a second batch of hamburgers on the grill to replace the first. Glancing at the plates on the table, he gestured at the offering. "Eat!" It was definitely an order.

Marina made no move to obey. "What about you?"

"I'll grab a couple from the next batch," Anderson promised. When he glanced back at her again, he saw that Marina was breaking apart the first hamburger she'd slipped onto her plate. "Looking for something?" he asked. "I've got to warn you, there are no hidden prizes inside the burgers."

"I thought the prize *was* the burger," she deadpanned.

He looked over at the infant a little skeptically. Sydney was back in her car seat, which in turn was on a chair beside her mother. "Isn't she too young for solid food?"

"Not my kid," Marina told him. "Sydney's been eating some solid foods since she was a little old lady of four months."

"And she's all right with it?" he asked, still skeptical. "I mean, there aren't any ill effects of her eating solid food at such a young age? Or am I just showing my ignorance about what babies can and can't do?"

"No ignorance," Marina told him. "You haven't been around babies very much, so how would you know?" she asked. "For the record, baby and doctor are both fine with it, as long as the food's pureed. Do you have a blender around? It's okay if you don't. I did bring a couple of jars of pureed fruit with me, but I'm pretty confident that she'd enjoy something different."

"Got one right there on the counter," he pointed out. "It's a gift from Paige, actually. She likes to mix herself these awful green smoothies when she comes by."

Marina got to work and had a small portion ready for her daughter within a few minutes.

As she carefully fed the baby, Marina took a bite of her own hamburger. She paused, savoring it.

"Hey, this *is* very good," she told Anderson, surprised.

"Told you," Jake piped up.

"Yes, you did," she agreed, "but most guys like to brag about their dads. That doesn't always mean what they're saying is true," she qualified.

"I wouldn't lie to you, Ms. Laramie," Jake told her with solemnity.

"And I appreciate that," Marina assured him, trying to keep a straight face. Her eyes shifted to Anderson again. He had finished making the second batch and was just sitting down at the table opposite her. "These are very, very good."

Her compliment pleased him, although his expression remained impassive. "Glad you like them."

She took another bite. Maybe it was her imagination, but it tasted even better than the first bite. "What did you put into them?" she marveled.

Anderson shrugged. "A little bit of this, a little bit of that."

She'd been a teacher long enough to know evasiveness when she heard it. "You're not going to give me your recipe?"

"Not a chance," he answered with a laugh. And then he looked at his son. "And you, you're sworn to secrecy."

Jake looked really surprised. "I am?"

"Yes, you are," Anderson told him with a straight face. The so-called secret was no big deal, but this was a way to test the boy's loyalties, he thought. "As of right now."

"Oh." Jake looked as if he was digesting this new piece of information. "I guess that means that Ms. Laramie and Sydney are just going to have to come over again if she wants to have your hamburgers, right, Dad?"

He was putting his father on the spot, Marina thought. She didn't want the day to turn awkward, not after they'd all been having such a nice time. She quickly came to Anderson's rescue.

"I don't think you should make your dad feel like he has to invite us back, Jake. It's up to him to extend the invitation—when he feels like it. Right now, I think he should have a chance to recover from our visit at his own pace."

She was trying to get him off the hook, Anderson realized. That made it easier for him to say yes to his son—and himself in the bargain.

"Well, if you ask me, I think that Jake's got a very good idea—unless, of course, you and Sydney have a lot of plans for the next few weeks," he added, not wanting Marina to think he was pressuring her into anything.

Jake turned his soulful eyes on his teacher and said, "You don't have any plans for the next few weeks, do you, Ms. Laramie?"

Marina looked from the son to the father, a smile budding and blooming on her lips. "Well, apparently I do now."

"Then you'll come?" Jake asked excitedly, grinning in total, unabashed glee.

"Yes." Her answer was given not just to Jake but to his father, as well. Maybe even foremost.

"When?" Jake was asking her, his wide blue eyes trained on her.

She gave him a completely innocent look. "That's entirely up your dad," she told him.

She didn't have to wonder long, because Anderson spoke up. "How about next Saturday?" he asked.

"Saturday sounds fine," she answered, delighted. Sydney made a funny little noise. Marina put her own spin on it. "Saturday's fine with Sydney, too," she told the Dalton men.

"Saturday it is," Anderson confirmed, allowing himself a very infectious smile.

"Want any more?" Anderson asked her after she had wound up consuming a second burger with as much enthusiasm as she had spent on the first.

"Only if you want to watch me explode," Marina protested. "I am really, really full." She glanced over at her daughter, who was dozing once again in her car seat. "And so is Sydney, from the looks of it."

Rising to her feet, Marina began gathering the plates.

Watching her for a moment, Anderson asked, "What are you doing?"

It wasn't exactly a mystery, she thought. Still, she answered politely, "I'm clearing the table."

"You don't have to," Anderson protested.

"I know," she answered matter-of-factly. "But I want to. It's the least I can do in appreciation for your hospitality." She looked over at Jake. "Want to help clean the plates?"

Jake jumped to his feet as if he was a jack-in-the-box in training. "Sure," he responded. The single word throbbed with verve.

Anderson continued observing her. He couldn't help admiring the way Marina could get his son to all but trip over himself in an effort to do her bidding.

She made it all look so effortless, he thought. Of course, the fact that Jake had a crush on her the size of Texas didn't exactly hurt her cause.

Still, it wasn't so much her face—which was damn pretty, he thought—as her personality that motivated his son. He was certain of it. Marina had a way about her that just seemed to pull a guy in, no matter what the age.

He was going to have to watch that himself, Anderson thought.

Although, after what he'd been through with Jake's mother, Lexie, he felt rather confident that when it came to matters that concerned women, he was rather savvy in that department. He wasn't about to be smitten, or led blindly around because of some sort of a surface attraction. The days of his being a gullible sucker who could be taken in by a pretty face were definitely over.

He had become a man who was suspicious of everyone and everything. Including sexy fifth-grade teachers.

"We had a wonderful time," Marina told Anderson later that evening as she stopped at her front door. Anderson was right beside her, his arms full of Sydney's car seat—and Sydney. Turning around, she smiled at him. "Thank you."

The day had turned out to be far more pleasant than he'd anticipated when he'd initially given Jake the go-ahead.

"It was our pleasure, right, Jake?" He looked at the boy, who was right beside him.

"Right!" Jake declared with feeling. He

looked up at Marina hopefully. "And you are coming next Saturday, like you said, right?"

Marina solemnly drew a cross over her heart. "I never go back on my word."

Anderson noticed that she hadn't directly answered his son's question. Looking at the sleeping infant in his arms, he made use of an excuse that had suddenly occurred to him,

"Jake, Sydney left her hat in the car. Do me a favor and get it for her."

"Sure thing," Jake said just before he took off.

He waited until he was sure the boy was out of earshot and then he spoke. "I don't want you to feel you have to come next Saturday if you don't want to."

She laughed, amused. "Funny, I was going to tell you that you shouldn't feel pressured into inviting us over next Saturday if you'd rather not."

He looked at her in confusion. "What gave you the idea that I feel pressured?"

She would have thought that *that* was self-evident. "Well, for one thing, Jake didn't exactly leave you any leeway."

He nodded his head, giving her the point. And then raising one of his own. "I could point out the same thing in your case."

That surprised her. "I don't feel any pressure."

"Neither do I," he replied—and then found himself getting lost in her smile.

"Then I guess we'll see each other Saturday," Marina told him.

Anderson nodded his head ever so slightly. "I guess so."

Had Jake not popped up just then, Sydney's hat in his hand, Anderson would have given in to the sudden impulse that came over him to kiss Marina.

Lucky for him, Jake did pop up just then, Anderson thought.

The thing was, he didn't exactly feel all that lucky about it.

Chapter 11

It was getting to be a habit, coming to Anderson's ranch, Marina thought as she watched Jake play peekaboo with Sydney. A habit she had to admit that she looked forward to, maybe even a little more each time than the last.

She told herself not to, that she shouldn't—but that didn't change things. The rest of the week couldn't go by fast enough for her.

This was their third weekend here—the invitation had been extended from just one day to two. In order to keep everything light and friendly, she and Sydney went home each Saturday night, only to return the following morning, even though Jake had innocently pointed out that it would be easier on her if she and her daughter just stayed on the ranch and spent the night.

And, she also had to admit, they were becoming closer. All of them. Although she had always tried to keep her professional life separated from her personal one, there was no way she could deny that she and Jake were getting closer.

As far as she and Jake's father went, well, nothing was said but she could *feel* the barriers between them disintegrating. Despite all her promises to herself never to allow another man to get close enough to touch her soul, she knew it was happening with Anderson. Seeing his kindness to her daughter and watching the way he acted toward his son had done that—penetrated her once-impenetrable shield without so much as firing a single shot at it.

"Ms. Laramie." The way Jake said her name made her realize that he'd already said it more than once and was now trying very hard to get her attention.

"Sorry," Marina apologized. "I was thinking about something and I guess I just didn't hear you. My mistake. What did I miss?"

"That's okay, Ms. Laramie." The look on the boy's face told her that he would forgive her anything. "I just wanted to know if it was okay with you to give Sydney a ride in my wagon." He indicated the bright red, shiny wagon that Anderson had brought out to the corral earlier. "I'll prop her up in her car seat and I'll go real slow," Jake promised.

"Let me secure the car seat first," Anderson interjected, taking part in the negotiations. "I've got some rope in the barn—if it's all right with you," he qualified, looking at Marina.

She had to admit that the prospect of what Jake was suggesting made her a little nervous, but she also knew that she couldn't allow her overprotectiveness to get in the way of Sydney experiencing things.

"And you're sure you'll go slowly?" Marina asked the boy.

Jake nodded his head so hard, it looked as if it was bobbing. "Like a poky old turtle," he told her, drawing a cross over his heart.

Marina laughed. She knew he was saying that for her benefit. "That doesn't sound like it'll be all that much fun for you."

The corners of Jake's eyes crinkled. "Oh, it will be," he assured her, then confided, "I like hearing Sydney laugh."

Marina smiled and tousled his hair fondly. "So do I, Jake, so do I." It was little details like this that had allowed Jake to seep into her heart. "There's nothing sweeter than the sound of innocent laughter."

Anderson came out carrying what looked to be a leather harness instead of the rope he'd gone to fetch.

"I think this'll work better in the long run," he told Marina and then proceeded to secure Sydney's car seat to his son's wagon with the leather straps. Testing it to make sure that it wouldn't suddenly come loose or that the wagon wouldn't wind up tipping over if Jake pulled on the leather too hard, Anderson stepped back and looked at his handiwork, a satisfied expression on his face.

"You're good to go, Jake," he informed his son.

In response, Jake looked down at the infant in his wagon. "Here we go, Sydney. Hang on!" And then he looked up in Marina's direction and lowered his voice in order to tell her, "I just said that to get her excited. I'll go slowly, like I promised."

The moment he began to pull the wagon, Sydney squealed with what sounded like sheer delight.

The whole scene completely warmed Marina's heart.

She moved back, standing beside Anderson to watch her daughter being pulled along by her student.

Sydney made another happy noise.

"You know," Marina said to the man beside her, thinking of the way her daughter had lit up this morning when she'd put her in her car seat and began to head out to the Dalton ranch, "if I didn't know any better, I'd have to say that Sydney really looks forward to these outings on your ranch."

Anderson was trying his best to concentrate on watching the children and blocking out his acute awareness of just how close he was standing to Marina.

He was also trying to block out the scent of her disturbingly arousing perfume before it completely undid him. He was also trying to deal with recurring, rather urgent thoughts that kept insisting on popping up in his head. Thoughts that had absolutely nothing to do with either his child or hers.

Just her.

He had to get a tighter rein on himself, Anderson thought impatiently, silently upbraiding himself.

"She's not the only one," Anderson replied, focusing strictly on what she had just said.

The next moment, when Marina looked at him quizzically, he realized what his words must have sounded like to her. He didn't want Marina thinking he was coming on to her, especially when he was busy fighting those very inclinations.

"I mean Jake." He cleared his throat, then continued, "I was talking about Jake's looking forward to you and Sydney coming over."

She'd been wrong, Marina thought, thinking that Anderson might actually have some small, budding feelings for her. She'd misread each and every sign.

Marina felt like an idiot. She searched for a way to save a little face, as well as a shred of her own self-esteem.

"You're a good father," she told him, doing her best to sound natural, yet somewhat removed, "putting up with things just to make Jake happy."

"Things?" Anderson echoed. She'd lost him again. He was getting better at understanding female-speak, but right now, he wasn't following her train of thought. Just what was she talking about?

"Well, yes." When she saw that Anderson still didn't seem to understand her subtle reference, she patiently spelled it out for him. "Sydney and me."

It took Anderson a couple of seconds to put two and two together. She thought he didn't want her here, he thought, astonished.

"What makes you think I'm 'putting up' with you?" He knew that he wasn't exactly the warm, outgoing type, but he was fairly certain that he hadn't said anything to offend her—or at least, he hadn't meant to offend her.

Marina looked at him. Did the man actually need it spelled out for him, or was he just pretending to be clueless? Since men could very easily *be* clueless, she gave him the benefit of the doubt.

"Well, you just went to some great lengths to make it clear that it was Jake who was looking forward to our visits. What that implies is that you *aren't* looking forward to them." She looked at him, daring Anderson to contradict that.

For his part, Anderson could only stare at her incredulously. How the hell had she arrived at that conclusion? Especially since the exact opposite was true—and that in itself was what really worried him. He had caught himself looking forward to Marina's visits—and he knew that ultimately wasn't good.

"You're putting words into my mouth," he told her with a touch of annoyance—then softened his tone just a tad. He didn't want her thinking he was some surly ogre, easily offended by the use of the wrong word. "Trust me, if I didn't want you here, I would have said so—and you *wouldn't* have been here."

Marina looked at him, trying to comprehend what Anderson was actually telling her. She was getting some very mixed signals.

A small frown curved the corners of her mouth as Marina tried to get what was going on straight in her mind.

"So you're not not looking forward to our visits?" she concluded. She watched his expression to see if she'd guessed correctly.

"Isn't that some kind of a double negative? Those are supposed to cancel each other out, right?" he asked, then went on to confess almost a little sheepishly, "Grammar wasn't exactly my best subject in school."

That had to have been hard for him to admit, Marina realized. The man had a great deal of pride. She did what she could to put him at ease.

"It usually isn't anybody's best subject," she told her host. "But yes, to answer your question, a double negative does cancel itself out, making the answer a positive one."

He nodded, appreciating that she hadn't

talked down to him when it could have been so easy for her to do that, given her educational background.

"I thought so," Anderson murmured, then went on to say a little more audibly, "And for the record, I do like having you come by with the baby. I enjoy watching her light up and respond to riding on Fury and the dozen and a half other things she's been encountering."

He looked a little wistful. "I missed all that with Jake," he told Marina, not entirely realizing that he was allowing the sadness he felt over that to come through. "Missed watching him grow, watching him respond to things for the first time." His expression grew even more wistful as he spoke. "All the things that parents wind up taking for granted I never got to experience. I guess I'm trying to recapture that by watching Sydney do all those 'firsts.'"

Anderson paused for a moment, as if weighing whether or not to say what he wanted to say next. "And I guess that I really feel as if I'd been cheated," he admitted bluntly.

His words touched her. She knew how she'd feel if for some reason, her daughter had been withheld from her and she'd been unable to take part in Sydney's formative years.

Her empathy for what Anderson had to be going through grew.

As she watched Jake slowly make his way to the far end of the corral, she lightly touched Anderson's arm to get his attention—and just maybe to form a little more of a bond.

When he turned his head to look at her, Marina said, "I know it won't begin to make up for it, but feel free to experience as much as you can with Sydney."

He had no idea what made him do what he did next. Maybe it was motivated by what Marina had just said, or maybe it was the look in her eyes, a mixture of sympathy and understanding.

Or maybe it was just the woman, standing beside him at the right time, the right place.

Most likely, it was a combination of all of that plus the ache of loneliness that seemed to have taken up permanent residence in his chest. Surrounded by his siblings, his son and the rest of his extended family, not to mention being involved with more physical labor than he could shake a proverbial stick at, by evening's end he still felt very much alone—with the prospect of remaining that way.

It wasn't a prospect that filled him with any sort of even mild joy.

Most of the time, he could put up with it, block it from his mind or ignore it outright. But right now, at this moment, it was different. Right now, that loneliness ate up his oxygen and punched holes in his resolve.

And before he knew what he was doing, that loneliness was making him do it. Making him take Marina into his arms and bring his mouth down to her very tempting one.

It was, he realized, as if he had no choice in the matter. As if somewhere, in some giant book in the sky, this was written down as being inevitable, as needing to happen in order for the rest of the world to go on spinning on its axis.

Because if he didn't do this, if he didn't kiss her, then the world as it existed, as everyone knew it, would cease to be.

Anderson truthfully didn't know who was more caught off guard and surprised by the action—him, or Marina.

What he was even more surprised at was that Marina didn't pull away. On the contrary, she seemed to melt right into him, as if she had been waiting for this, as if she had known, once it happened, that it *had* to happen.

The second their lips touched, he was completely undone. Marina tasted exactly as he knew she would. She tasted of everything wondrous, spellbinding and life-affirming. And something akin to strawberries.

And he wanted more.

So very much more than he could have right at this moment.

Anderson heard her moan against his lips and excitement shot up through the roof, going from high up to completely immeasurable.

All he knew was that it was completely off the charts and far more disturbing and yet more wonderful than anything he had ever experienced or even could possibly anticipate experiencing.

He knew he should stop. A grown man would have called a halt to this even before it had begun—or at the very least, a moment after it had started.

But all he wanted to do was hang in there—hang on for dear life and savor the completely uncharted territory he had fallen, headfirst, into.

The thought gave him no peace. He had to stop. Now, before it got out of hand. Before his son made it back to where he had started his journey and saw him lip-locked with his teacher. He knew how Jake felt about his teacher—the boy had a huge crush on her—

and he didn't want to be the source of heartache for his son.

A second longer, Anderson told himself, just one tiny second longer.

He wanted to remain lost in her kiss for just a second longer and then he'd pull away. No harm in letting this continue just a couple of heartbeats longer, right?

Or maybe longer than that?

"Dad, are you and Ms. Laramie getting married?" Jake asked excitedly.

And just like that, the question shattered the exquisite moment he had been sharing with Marina.

Chapter 12

He didn't remember doing it, didn't remember separating himself from the woman he'd just been kissing. One moment his lips were firmly pressed against hers, the next, with his son's voice ringing in his head, Anderson found himself suddenly springing away from her as if he'd just been poked—hard—by a cattle prod.

Flushing, struggling to regain his bearings, Anderson looked down at his son.

"What?" And then the boy's question replayed itself in his head. "No," he cried with feeling.

The word vibrated with such intensity that

Marina felt as if she'd just been roughly slapped by the man who had just seconds earlier stirred such a wondrous kaleidoscope of feelings in her head. Feelings and sensations that caused her, just for that single instant, to actually forget all the promises that she'd made to herself regarding ever, *ever* letting her guard down.

She'd forgot that she wasn't supposed to.

But the abrupt coldness in Anderson's heartfelt denial that there was anything remotely in the offing as far as their future went swiftly brought reality crashing down all around her.

Marina felt as if she was suddenly standing in a field of ashes.

Somehow, she managed to recover, not for her own sake, but for Jake's. She'd heard the note of hope in the boy's voice. She didn't want him crushed—or led astray.

"Your father's right, dear," she assured the boy, sounding a little formal in order to keep her hurt from breaking through.

"Then why was he kissing you?" Jake wanted to know, regarding them suspiciously, as if he wasn't sure whether or not his father was telling him the truth.

"People kiss without getting married, Jake," she told him, her voice deliberately breezy. "It happens all the time." She spared Anderson a look. "It doesn't mean a thing."

Anderson couldn't tell if she was letting him off the hook because of Jake, or if she was really being serious and putting him on notice that the kiss had meant less than nothing to her.

Either way, he knew he should be relieved—except he wasn't. He felt guilty because he was fairly certain that there were still hurt feelings involved. He was really sorry if there were, but there was nothing he could do about that—at least not without compromising himself in front of his son.

This was getting way too complicated. He had more than he could handle just trying to navigate these new turbulent fatherhood waters. He had no room for the kind of baggage having a girlfriend created. Never mind that she could be something more than that, that somewhere in his misbegotten soul he might even *want* her to be more than that.

Get a grip, man. If you're not careful, you'll be going down for the third time.

Apparently, despite his teacher's disclaimer and the look on his father's face, Jake chose to see things from a different perspective.

"Oh, I don't know, it already feels like you

and Dad, Sydney and me are this big happy family," he declared happily.

"Sydney and I, not Sydney and me," Marina corrected him.

But Jake was focused on the bigger picture and not something as mundane as grammar that needed correcting. His eyes lit up. "Then you agree!" Jake exclaimed gleefully.

This was getting away from her. "No, no, I'm just trying to get you to speak correctly, I didn't mean to imply that what you said was right," Marina told him helplessly.

The grin on the boy's face told her that he wasn't buying what she was telling him. It was as if he could see through all the camouflage straight down to the heart of the matter.

"Whatever you say, Ms. Laramie." He all but winked as he pretended to agree with her. Sydney was making gurgling noises and Jake looked at his lone passenger. "I think she's hungry," he announced to the two adults. "Maybe we should go back inside the house and have some lunch before she gets cranky."

Marina slanted a glance at Anderson as Jake began to head toward the house with Sydney. "Is it my imagination, or did he suddenly become the adult?"

Anderson blew out a frustrated breath as

his son walked away. "Jake certainly became something," he reluctantly agreed.

But his mind wasn't on Jake; it was on his own foolish slip. Kissing Marina had turned the ground beneath his feet to quicksand. But he wasn't going to allow himself to get sucked in again, the way he had with Lexie. Pairing up with Lexie had been a total mistake. He'd thought she was a mild-mannered and agreeable woman, only to discover that she was actually a self-centered creature with her own agenda. An agenda that had had little regard for him as a person, much less any regard for his feelings.

Though he wouldn't admit it to anyone, not even his own family, because of Lexie's deception his ego and self-esteem were still very bruised and in serious need of repair. He couldn't risk going through something like that again, not if he wanted to survive. And he *had* to survive, had to do right by his son. Jake's welfare was the only thing that mattered to him. It wasn't just himself he had to think about anymore. He had Jake to consider and put before anything else—and that definitely included putting the boy before his own self-gratification.

All he had to do to get through this afternoon, Anderson told himself, was to avoid making direct eye contact with Marina.

Easier said than done.

For the remainder of the visit, Marina did her best to act as if nothing had changed. But something definitely had.

Two somethings, actually, she thought. The first thing that had changed—and foremost in her mind—was that Anderson had kissed her. Not just a peck on the cheek or a quick, stolen kiss that was over before it had actually even begun, but a long, toe-curling, soul-changing, mind-blowing kiss that had changed the parameters of the world as she knew it.

The second, which she had a sneaking suspicion was a direct result of the first, was that she was acutely aware that for the remainder of the visit, Anderson had withdrawn from her and from the visit in general.

His interactions with her, with her daughter and even with his son were cut down to monosyllabic responses that were given in answer to any questions directed to him.

That was the act of a man who was troubled by something he had either done or was about to do. Marina had her suspicions that it was a combination of both. She tried very hard not to dwell on it and consequently, she was unable to do anything else *but* dwell on it, even though she did her best to put up a good front. She did the latter for Jake's sake because she didn't want him thinking something was wrong until that conclusion was absolutely unavoidable.

She did her best to hold it at bay as long as she could.

Because she didn't want to push her luck—or to have some sort of a confrontation suddenly erupt between Anderson and her—Marina called an early end to their time together.

The event did not go unnoticed.

"But you never leave this early," Jake protested when she announced right after she had cleared away the dishes that she and Sydney had had a lovely time, but now they had to be going home.

Marina had been afraid of this reaction from Jake, but it didn't change her mind.

"I know, honey, but Sydney's tired and I think she might be coming down with a cold. It's best if I get her home and put her to bed." She assumed that was the end of it, but she should have known better.

"We've got beds here," Jake volunteered. "Lots of beds. You could put her to bed here and maybe she'll feel better, right, Dad?" he asked, turning toward Anderson and waiting for his father to back him up.

But he was disappointed. "Jake, if Ms. Laramie wants to take Sydney home and put her to bed, she has a right to do that."

Jake looked crestfallen. "I know, but—"

He hated saying no to Jake, but this was for both their good.

"Never argue with a guest, Jake," Anderson told his son, draping a restraining arm around the boy's shoulders. "Ms. Laramie wants to take Sydney home, so we should let her do that."

The wording about the argument clearly went over Jake's head. "I thought I was arguing with you," Jake told his dad.

"Never do that, either," Marina said softly, adding her voice to the discussion and coming to Anderson's aid. "Being a dad is hard, Jake. It involves doing things that aren't always popular, but that still need to be done anyway."

Jake's face was puckered as he tried to make sense of what he was being told. It was obvious that he was having very little luck with that. Reluctantly, he gave in. "Okay—if you say so, Ms. Laramie."

Gathering her things together, Marina paused for a moment to run her hand along

Jake's cheek. "You are a sweet, sweet boy, Jake. Your dad's very lucky to have you as his son," she told him.

The next moment, she snapped out of her mood and went back to gathering everything together. It seemed to her that each time she left, there were more things to take back with her—certainly more than she had brought in the first place. She looked around carefully, making sure she had everything. An uneasiness told her that she wouldn't be coming back.

As usual, Jake was right behind her, carrying as much as his short arms could hold.

And Anderson was behind him, bringing up the rear.

That, too, wasn't unusual, not in itself. He always helped her carry things to her car, but there was never this reserved air about him when he was doing it, the way there was today.

He wasn't saying a word, wasn't joining in the conversation the way he normally did. Instead, he was acting as if he was the odd man out, excluded by choice from the club of two formed by his son and his son's teacher—the woman who had, for one brief shining moment, turned his entire world upside down.

But that world had to be righted and he was determined to be the one to do it.

Jake was shifting from foot to foot, as if he was doing some strange little happy dance that only he was privy to.

"I can't wait for the week to go by and next Saturday to come," Jake confided. "I'm going to have something special planned for Sydney," he announced happily.

"Oh? What?" Marina asked, trying her hardest to be upbeat, telling herself that she was only imagining Anderson's sudden change in behavior, that she was reading things into it when there was really nothing there to read.

Maybe the thought of being happy worried her. It brought with it its own set of demons that needed to be dealt with. The last time she recalled being too happy for words, it hadn't been long before her world came crashing down around her.

"Can't tell you," Jake answered. "'Cause if I did, then it wouldn't be a surprise for Sydney."

"I promise I won't tell her," Marina said solemnly, crossing her heart for him.

Despite that, Jake was determined to keep the surprise to himself and spring it on Sydney the following weekend.

He shook his head from side to side. "Sorry, I can't tell you. I don't want you to be tempted," he said, sounding for all the world as if he was an adult.

Marina secured Sydney's car seat in the back of her vehicle. Just before she got into her car herself, Marina turned toward Anderson and said, "Thank you for having us over again." Her gaze met his and she added with feeling, "Sydney and I had a wonderful time," even as she wondered if this was the last time she would be standing here like this.

Anderson met her words of thanks with a shrug. If she didn't know any better, she would have said that he looked relieved to see her leaving with her daughter.

"Glad you could come." He said it with as much feeling as he would have exhibited talking about his last month's telephone bill.

There was nothing left to do but leave.

Marina ruffled Jake's hair just before getting in behind the wheel. "See you bright and early in school tomorrow, young man."

Jake's eyes fairly sparkled. "You bet," he cried happily.

He hung on his father's arm as he watched the vehicle drive down the winding road. He watched until he couldn't see it anymore.

And then he had a question. "Why do you think she had to leave so early, Dad?"

Because she knows it's better this way, Anderson thought. Out loud, he addressed Jake's question. "She said it was because she was worried Sydney was coming down with a cold, remember?"

But it was obvious that Jake didn't believe that. He shook his head. "I don't think so. Sydney didn't sneeze or cough."

Anderson found himself wishing that the boy wasn't as insightful as he apparently was. "She's still the baby's mother, Jake. It's best not to interfere in family matters."

Jake sighed and then nodded. "If you say so, Dad." Turning toward the house, he began to take off.

"Where are you going in such a hurry?" Anderson wanted to know. He wasn't accustomed to seeing his son moving so fast once it was just the two of them.

Jake paused just long enough to answer him. "I thought I'd start working on Sydney's surprise for next week."

Anderson thought of the phone call he was going to make in a little while. "Maybe you should hold off on that for a few days."

Jake stared at him for a long moment, as if trying to come to some sort of a conclusion about what his father was telling him. But after a moment, it was obvious that none had been reached.

"Why, Dad?"

He hated being put on the spot this way, hated being the one to cause his son any disappointment. But some things had to be done in the name of self-preservation. This was one of them.

"You never know when something might just go wrong, Jake. Maybe Ms. Laramie won't be able to make it next week."

But Jake shook his head. "Nothing's going to happen," he said with such total conviction, it gave Anderson pause.

But not for long.

She almost didn't pick up her phone when it rang. She certainly knew she didn't want to.

The caller ID told her that Anderson was on the line and her intuition told her she wasn't going to like what he had to say. So, for reasons of self-preservation, she almost let her machine pick it up.

But that, Marina told herself, was only putting off the inevitable. The longer she did that, the worse it would wind up being for her. So, putting her daughter down in the port-a-crib she kept for Sydney in her living room, Marina picked up the receiver.

"Hello?" she asked almost hesitantly.

"Marina," she heard the deep voice rumble in her ear, "this is Anderson Dalton."

"I know," she replied quietly, "I have caller ID. Besides, I recognize your voice. Is something wrong with Jake? Did something happen to him?" she asked, wanting to get that out of the way first. After all, it wasn't entirely inconceivable that Anderson might be calling about his son.

"No, Jake's fine," he assured her.

So much for a final desperate grasp at an excuse, she thought. "Good." Lord, this felt oddly painful, she couldn't help thinking. More painfully awkward than their first exchange that time he came storming into her classroom after hours.

Marina gathered her courage to her. "Why are you calling, then? Did I forget something back at your place?"

"No." He paused for a moment before continuing. "But I did."

Okay, he'd lost her, she thought. "I don't understand."

"I forgot not to get involved. And I am. Getting involved," he tacked on. "So I think it's best for everyone's sake if we stop getting together over the weekends."

Even though she'd tried to prepare herself for this, she felt as if someone had twisted her heart right out of her chest.

"Does Jake know?" she asked quietly.

"Jake doesn't have to know about it," Anderson said curtly. "I'm the one who make the decisions."

Then act like an adult and tell me what's going on, she wanted to shout. Instead, she said, "I know, but I just thought that since he's so involved with us coming over—"

Desperate, Anderson went to his initial go-to excuse. "People are starting to talk."

"People?" she echoed, momentarily lost. What was he talking about? "What people?"

"People-people," he said in exasperation. "You're Jake's teacher, I'm his father. I don't want anything being said or done that might compromise your job there—or my son's education. Jake needs you too much as his teacher."

"So this is about him."

Her voice was very still. Was Anderson actually trying to get her to believe that he was sacrificing something they might have in order to stop some perceived gossip that hadn't happened yet? Marina doubled her fist at her side.

"Absolutely—and your reputation."

And it has nothing to do with you running scared, she added silently. Out loud she said, "Well, I appreciate you being so concerned about my reputation, Anderson." Her voice was crisp, removed.

"Don't mention it," Anderson said, hanging up before she could say anything else that would make him lose his nerve.

He'd almost lost it twice already.

Chapter 13

"I know what you're thinking."

Marina said the words out loud as she glanced at her daughter. Sydney's huge blue eyes were following her as she moved around the small apartment, trying, through sheer force of will, to somehow fill up the overwhelming emptiness and find a space for herself.

"I said I'd never be in this position again, never leave myself wide open so I could hurt like this again. And yet, here I am, doing it to myself all over again, just like the first time." Marina took in a deep breath, trying to center herself. "But it's not like Jake's dad made any promises to me, not the way I felt that your father did. You wouldn't remember him," she assured the infant. "He was gone before you were born—his loss, honey. All that means is that I'm going to love you twice as much—if that's possible." She never wanted Sydney to feel unlovable the way she had because of her father's absences. Granted, things had changed of late. Hank Laramie had come back into her sister Dawn's life and into hers, apparently wanting to make amends.

All that was well and good, but it was going to take a long time for the emptiness she'd felt while she was growing up to finally fade away. She wasn't emotionally up to taking on something more only to be disappointed. Thinking that it would be different with Anderson was a mistake. She needed to be grateful that she hadn't gone any further, hadn't made an even bigger mistake with the man.

Get over it, Marina, she told herself.

Marina blew out a breath as she sat down on the sofa. She could still feel Sydney's eyes on her. She looked down at her daughter, who, lying in her port-a-crib, was parked on the floor directly in front of the sofa.

She needed to talk this out of her system, she thought.

"But Jake's dad, well," she said wistfully, "I

was really beginning to think that you and I had a future with him. He's trying really hard to be a good dad to Jake and I could tell he had a weakness for you—who wouldn't?" she asked with a laugh. "So all that seemed really promising to me. A lot of guys run when fatherhood is sprung on them."

And she would be the first to testify to that, Marina thought, remembering the expression on Gary's face the evening she had told him that she was pregnant with his baby.

"And when Anderson kissed me, Sydney," she said, reliving the very intense moment, "Oh, when he kissed me, I thought that we were both on to something very special. Something with promise." She sighed as she picked up the remote control from the side table. "I guess I just let my imagination get carried away."

Turning on the flat-screen that hung on the wall across from her, Marina began trolling through the channels, searching for something that would be distracting enough to make her forget about the ever growing ache she felt.

"Anyway, it looks like it's going to be just you and me tonight, kidlet. What are you in the mood for?"

Sydney seemed to scrunch up her face and make an emphatic noise.

Marina put her own meaning to the sound. "Yeah, me, too. But Jake and his dad aren't coming over tonight. Or, probably, not tomorrow night or the night after that," she added, sadly. "But we'll get by, you and I." She tried to put as much positive energy into the statement as she could. "We did it before, we'll do it again."

As if in response, Sydney made another noise and Marina forced a resigned smile to her lips. "You're right. I don't believe me, either. But I'm going to give it a really good try. We're *not* going to let this bring us down."

She only hoped she could live up to those words.

It was a small town and, realistically, Marina knew that it was only to be expected that their paths would cross sometime or other. But, despite the fact that she was a full-time teacher and that Anderson was a full-time rancher, for some unknown reason, their paths seemed to be crossing *all* the time.

So much so that it seemed to be happening almost every day.

When Anderson came to pick up Jake or

when she made a quick stop at the supermarket, all she had to do was look up and there the man was, almost in her space. And, when she did look in his direction, she saw Anderson ducking his head down, pretending that he hadn't been looking her way.

The hell he wasn't.

It was a ridiculous game they were playing and they both knew it, she thought. And yet, they continued playing it.

The first time she'd accidentally run into Anderson, it was because she'd noticed that one of her students—Hannah McKay—had left her math book on her desk. Since the girl needed the book in order to do the assigned math homework that night, Marina had grabbed it and hurried after the girl, who had left the classroom, along with the other students, less than five minutes earlier.

Hurrying from the classroom, Marina had dashed out into the hallway and out the front door—straight into Anderson Dalton. She'd almost managed to knock both of them down from the force of the impact. Anderson had steadied himself at the last moment and automatic reflexes had him catching her by her shoulders before she fell.

For one prolonged second they looked at one

another, each surprised beyond words to see the other. Surprised and almost undone. It took another very long moment before they were able to recover themselves.

Marina did it first, bracing her shoulders and stiffening as she took a very deliberate step back, away from him.

"Sorry," she apologized almost woodenly, "I didn't mean to almost knock you down. I was in a hurry to catch—Hannah!" she called, seeing the girl and trying to get her attention. "I'm sorry," she apologized again, pulling herself entirely out of Anderson's hold. "I need to give this to her."

She held the book aloft as if to offer proof that her story was genuine and not just a mere desperate fabrication.

With that, she pulled herself away and quickly headed in the girl's direction.

Jake had been a stunned, silent witness to the whole thing.

"That was Ms. Laramie," he pointed out needlessly to his father.

Anderson's heart literally felt like lead in his chest as he replied, "Yes, I know."

"Don't you want to talk to her?" Jake asked with a barely veiled desperate note in his voice.

His eyes darted from his father to the teacher and then back again.

"Not particularly." It was a lie, but he forced himself to utter it. "I'd rather talk to you," Anderson said, draping an arm around his son's shoulders. "So how was today?"

Jake's momentary lighthearted display of exuberance, Anderson noticed, was conspicuously gone as Jake answered his question, prefacing it with a heavy sigh, "Okay, I guess."

And so began his son's rather pronounced downward spiral.

It grew, Anderson noticed, a little more intense with each day that passed. And, as those days went by, Anderson found himself questioning his own actions and his reasoning behind the path he had decided to take with Marina.

Maybe going this route did prevent him from making any kind of personal mistakes he might find himself regretting in the near future, but this route also seemed to be taking all the liveliness, all the energy out of Jake. Within one short week, they were suddenly back where they started from, with his being the parent of a robot who was far more connected to his video games than he was to him.

The light, Anderson had noticed, had gone out of Jake's eyes.

And then something happened that made his own actions and Jake's reactions to what he'd done seem to be totally moot.

Jake's mother, Lexie, showed up on his doorstep unannounced.

She came breezing up to the ranch just the same way she had when she'd decided— seemingly out of the blue—that Jake needed to spend some "quality time" with his father. That was when she'd just deposited the boy on his doorstep as if he was no more than a package that needed to be posted.

But this time when she showed up, she announced that she was here to take back what she had so carelessly left behind.

"That's right," she said to Anderson in no uncertain terms, "I've come to take Jake home."

Her bluntly stated intentions almost left him speechless. How could she just barrel in like a tornado and take away his son without so much as blinking her eyes? Didn't she realize how destructive that was for Jake's morale? Never mind how it affected him personally.

He tried his best to make her understand, to see beyond her own selfish point of view.

"But this is Jake's home now," Anderson protested.

The annoyed, exasperated expression on her face told Anderson just what the woman thought of his argument. Less than nothing.

"Correction, this was just someplace he was spending some time—until I came back for him. Well, I came back for him," she announced, as if that wasn't already painfully apparent.

Anderson fisted his hands at his sides to keep from wrapping them around her throat and strangling the selfish, thoughtless woman.

"He's not a football you can just punt back and forth," Anderson insisted.

Lexie looked at him as if he was babbling. "Of course he's not. Look, all I did was let him spend some time with you because you were so adamant about spending time with *him*," she concluded as if that answered everything.

"I was adamant a year ago," Anderson reminded her. "And you refused to let me have Jake. Why did you suddenly change your mind twelve months later?" he challenged.

Lexie shrugged her shoulders, a look of disinterested annoyance on her face. "Because I'm big enough to admit that I was wrong. A boy does need to spend some time with his father. But he's spent it and now I'm taking him back."

It all sounded too pat to him. Lexie was up to something; he'd bet his soul on it.

"Is that the only reason?" he asked, pinning her with a look. "And I warn you, there are ways to find out if you're telling me the truth."

Lexie blew out a breath, her hands on her hips. He could see the frustration clearly on her face, no doubt because nothing was going according to her plans. She was a woman who was used to things falling into her lap the way she had hoped. But not this time.

The frustration boiled over and Lexie snapped. "I wanted to spend some quality time with Raul, okay?" she said, telling him the real reason for Jake's sudden transplant earlier in July.

"Raul?" Anderson echoed, confused. "Who the hell is Raul?"

"Raul is history," Lexie answered with finality, "so there's no point in talking about him. What's important here is that I'm putting you on notice," she emphasized. "I want my son back and I'm going to take him with me. Now be a good soldier," she ordered sarcastically, "and tell Jake so that he's ready to go back to Chicago in five days."

And with that, the woman breezed out again, leaving ashes and ruin in her wake.

Anderson stood looking after her, the words *five days* echoing over and over again in his head.

"Jake, if your face was any longer, we'd have to put cones around it to keep people from tripping on it," Marina pointed out kindly the following Monday morning.

The rest of the class had gone out for recess, but Jake, she'd noticed, remained where he was, staring off into space and completely oblivious to what was going on around him.

Marina made her way over to his row and sat down in the seat right in front of the boy. The haunted, sad expression on his face tore at her heart.

Turning around in order to face him, she asked in a kindly voice, "What's wrong, Jake?"

Jake refused to look at her and kept staring off into space. But she could see the sheen of tears forming in his eyes.

"Nothing," he mumbled, saying the word so quietly, had she not been sitting right in front of him, she wouldn't have been able to hear it.

She was not about to give up and let him

have his space. This was too important and he was too tortured to leave alone.

"No, I know 'nothing' and this is definitely not 'nothing.' Now out with it," she ordered kindly. "You've been looking as if you lost your best friend or your beloved pet all morning long. Please tell me what's wrong."

Jake raised his eyes to hers and for a moment, she thought he was just going to maintain his silence on the subject.

But then he sighed.

It was a long, heartfelt sigh that seemed to come from the very depths of his toes and raked right over his heart. She could see that saying the words hurt him a great deal. "It's just that I'm not going to be here much longer."

This was the first time she was hearing this and it hit her with the force of a well-delivered punch to the stomach, stealing the very air out of her lungs.

"Oh? Why?" she asked, surprised. "Where are you going?" She wanted to know.

He was clearly miserable as he spoke, staring down at his shoes. It was as if his head felt too heavy to hold up.

"Mom says home, but it doesn't feel like it's home anymore. Is that weird?" he asked her, looking up. "I mean, I've been here just a couple of months and I've been there all my life, but when I think of 'home,' I think of here." The corners of his mouth turned completely down and for a moment, Marina thought that he was going to cry. But then he managed to hold himself together. "Except that I won't be here soon."

To say she was stunned was a vast understatement.

"Are you sure about this?" she asked Jake.

Jake bobbed his head up and down and his expression seemed to just grow sadder by degrees as he replied, "Yes, I'm sure. I heard Dad talking to Mom and she told him that she was taking me back. Ms. Laramie, I don't want to go," he told her plaintively. There was a hitch in his voice, as if he was doing his best not to cry. "Do I hafta?"

It wasn't her place to raise the boy's hopes, or to dash them, either. So, as much as she would have wanted to say something to bolster his morale, Marina forced herself to go for neutral ground.

"What does your dad say?" she asked him, fervently praying that Anderson had told the boy something she could expand on.

Again the small shoulders rose and fell. "He didn't say too much—and he looked kind of sad." Jake's eyes begged her to say something positive he could cling to.

There wasn't much to work with there, but she did her best. "That's because he doesn't want you to go."

The look on his face was just breaking her heart. "You think so?"

In her heart, she all but cursed Anderson for not promising the boy he could stay at his home until all appeals were exhausted—hopefully, by then, Jake's flaky mother would have lost interest in whatever game she was trying to play.

"Oh, I'm sure of it."

But Jake was not a boy to be easily fooled or put off. "Then why doesn't he tell Mom no?"

Although she hated to do it, Marina gave him a one-size-fits-all excuse. "I'm afraid it's not that simple, honey."

Jake refused to let it go. He fought to understand. His immediate future depended on it.

"Why not? I don't want to go and he doesn't want me to go. That's two against one, Ms. Laramie," he pointed out. "Doesn't that win?"

Oh, Jake, if only. "In a democracy," she said out loud, "yes, it does. But I'm afraid that this is different."

Jake clearly didn't understand—and he wanted to. "How?"

She smiled sadly at him as she caressed his cheek and shook her head. "If that were easy to answer, there wouldn't be any need for lawyers in this world, honey."

For the first time in a week, Jake's face lit up. "Dad says that my grandpa's a lawyer. Does that help any?" he asked hopefully.

"That's true," Marina said. "Well, then, maybe that *can* help," she told the boy. "Maybe your dad's going to talk to your grandpa to see if maybe there's a way to convince your mother to allow you to live here—or to at least let you stay until the end of the school year."

A small smile began to curve the corners of his mouth. "That would be good," Jake agreed. "Because I really like school, Ms. Laramie—and I really like coming to your class every day."

She could feel tears stinging her eyes. In such a short time, the boy had managed to burrow his way into her heart.

Like father, like son, she couldn't help thinking.

"Well, thank you, Jake. I really like having you as my student," she replied with feeling.

It was all that she would allow herself to

say at the moment. In her heart she knew that yanking Jake out of school just when he was finally getting adjusted to it would be doing a grave disservice to the boy, never mind what it would do to his father or the blow that Anderson would suffer in having to give the boy up again so soon after having finally gained what had seemed like at least partial custody of his son.

It made her wonder about the kind of woman Jake's mother was. Wonder, too, what Anderson could have seen in her in the first place. From what she understood, there had been no long-standing relationship that had turned sour. Instead, there had been a brief interlude and ten years later, Anderson was made aware— by accident—that the interlude had resulted in his son. A son that Jake's mother had no intentions of sharing—until she did.

The woman, Marina couldn't help thinking, had some very serious stability issues. But that wasn't really the point. The point of it—and of everything—was Jake's welfare and making Jake smile again.

She just had to come up with a way, Marina told herself—a way acceptable to everyone— to make that happen.

Chapter 14

Lexie went back on her word.

Anderson didn't know why that even mildly surprised him. After all, it wasn't as if the woman was exactly trustworthy. Initially, she had said that she was going to give Jake five days to get used to the idea of returning to Chicago before she came to get him.

But she didn't give Jake five days, she gave him three. Three days with no warning of what was about to happen.

Just like that, when he was sitting down to dinner with his son, Lexie descended on both of them like some dire, deadly form of the medieval black plague.

She knocked on the front door and when

Anderson opened the door, just like that, she made her announcement.

Pushing past him, Lexie looked around the room for their son. When she didn't see him immediately, she turned on Anderson and declared, "He's coming with me *now*."

Anderson stared at her, stunned. He continued holding the door open for a moment longer, hoping she would take the hint and leave.

She didn't.

"You said he had five days," Anderson protested, following her into the foyer.

Lexie's annoyed expression told him that she had no patience with any delaying tactics. "And now I'm saying he doesn't. Why does everything have to be an argument with you?" she demanded.

"I could say the same to you," Anderson shot back.

And then he caught a glimpse of Jake out of the corner of his eye. The boy had followed him out to the living room. Right now, Jake looked as if he was cowering in the wake of their raised voices.

Anderson forced himself to lower his. He wasn't doing Jake any good by fighting with Lexie this way and ultimately, the woman had the law on her side. She was Jake's mother and she was the one who had legal custody of the boy. He was going to do whatever he could to change that, but right at this moment, he knew the end result of tonight's confrontation: she'd take Jake with her.

The thought almost killed him.

"Let him stay the two days, Lexie. What harm could it do?" Anderson asked, trying to appeal to her sense of fair play—even though he was certain that she ultimately didn't have any.

"The 'harm' is that those are two extra days I have to hang around this flyspeck of a town instead of flying back to a civilized world. As it is, I've let you two play house longer than I should have. Now hear this. Playtime is over. I want my son and I want to go home," she bit off angrily. Her eyes narrowed as she demanded, "Make it happen."

Jake grabbed his arm imploringly as he all but hid on his other side, the side away from his mother. "Dad, please don't let her take me. I want to stay here with you and Ms. Laramie and Sydney. Please, Dad. *Please*," Jake begged.

It was as if someone had waved a red flag in front of Lexie. "Who the hell are Ms. Laramie and Sydney?" she demanded hotly. She turned on Anderson. "Just what kind of perverted carryings-on have you been having here, Anderson?"

He dug down deep for patience—and to hold on to his temper.

"Ms. Laramie is his teacher and Sydney is her little girl," he told her evenly, doling out each word one at a time. "Jake wants to feel like he's part of a family unit and they provide that for him."

He couldn't have said anything worse to her if he'd tried. Lexie's complexion reddened as her eyes flashed with anger.

"He *is* part of a family," she retorted, grabbing the boy's arm. "He's part of *my* family." Lexie huffed angrily. "I was crazy to let you have him," she declared. "Let's go, Jake," she ordered.

Jake tried to dig in his heels. "But my things—" he protested.

"Your father will send them," Lexie snapped. Holding on to his arm tightly, she all but dragged the boy to the door.

Anderson wanted to stop her, wanted to grab the boy and pull him away from this woman he regarded as a she-devil, but he refused to turn his son into the living embodiment of a game of tug-of-war.

So all he could do was appeal to her humanity, which was, he knew even as he did it, a completely lost cause. He did it anyway.

"Lexie, please don't do this."

"What I shouldn't have done," she informed him as she opened the front door, still tightly holding on to Jake, "was go out with you that night twelve years ago. *That's* what I shouldn't have done."

And with that, Lexie stormed out of the house with Jake in tow, slamming the door so hard behind her, it shook.

Rage ate away at him.

Anderson struggled with the almost over-powering urge to go after the woman and take back his son. But that wouldn't solve anything and if he knew Lexie, this would wind up with her getting the sheriff to come back with her and haul Jake away. The whole thing would be very traumatic for Jake and that wasn't something he wanted to do to the boy.

And, though it cost him dearly, he didn't want Jake hating his mother, either. At least not on his account.

But that still didn't keep him from wanting to strangle Lexie.

The palms of his hands itched.

The law offices of Ben Dalton were in a simple, tidy looking one story building near the center of town. The decor was on the masculine side and subtly inspired a feeling of confidence in the average person who walked through the front doors.

As Anderson came through those doors, he found himself hoping that there was something to that.

Nodding at the receptionist who presided over the office's centrally located front desk, Anderson asked, "Is my father in?"

"He has a meeting scheduled with a client in twenty minutes," she told him.

"Then I'll be quick," Anderson promised as he went past her, heading toward his father's office.

Knocking once, he walked in before his father could tell him to enter.

Ben Dalton, tall, distinguished-looking, with a hint of gray just beginning at his temples, wore his age well. He was blessed with a poker face, but he looked surprised to see his first-born. Anderson rarely made an appearance in his world.

"Something wrong on the ranch?" Ben wanted to know, saying the first thing that came to mind.

"Only in a general sense," Anderson answered. He paused for a second, trying to get his thoughts in order. His brain felt as if it had been haphazardly tossed in the air and he was having trouble thinking. "Technically, this has nothing to do with the ranch. Just with me," he added before finally making his appeal, "Dad, I need your help."

The slight crease in his brow was the only indication that Ben Dalton was concerned. Very concerned. "What is it?"

"I know that this isn't the kind of case you normally handle," Anderson prefaced, "but I need help in getting custody of my son."

Ben squared his shoulders just a tad. This was still a sore point between them, Anderson knew. Not that Anderson had a son, but that he had known he had one for a year and hadn't said anything to his father until the boy had suddenly turned up on the ranch, forcing introductions to be made.

Ben raised his chin. "You mean the grandson I didn't know about until just recently?"

Anderson pressed his lips together. He didn't want to get into that squabble right now. This was far more important. "Yes, that one."

Ben nodded, as if tucking what was being said into its proper corners. "Before we go on, is there anything else you're keeping from me?"

Anderson sighed. Obviously he wasn't going to be able to just set this aside until later. "Dad,

I didn't tell you about Jake when I found out because there wasn't anything I could do to even get Lexie to give me visitation rights. I thought telling you about a grandson you weren't even allowed to see was cruel, so I decided not to say anything." He set his mouth hard. "This isn't the time to make me pay for that."

"No," Ben agreed, "You're right, this isn't." He turned his attention to the immediate problem at hand. "It's going to be an uphill battle," he warned his son. "You don't need the extra pressure of my needling you. Let me ask around," Ben proposed, "and see what I can come up with." His face softened with understanding, as if speaking as one father to another. "She just appeared out of the blue and took him, huh?"

Anger creased his features. "Like he was a piece of forgotten luggage she swooped in to pick up," Anderson said in utter disgust.

Ben shook his head. "I certainly hope your taste in women has improved since then." Before Anderson could respond to that, he held up his hand to silence him. "While I'm looking into this, you might try running the details by your sister," Ben suggested.

Anderson's thoughts were still colliding into

one another. For a moment, he didn't follow his father. "Which one?"

"The one who's a lawyer," Ben prompted. "Now that she's graduated, Lindsay's joined the firm. She's already got a case," he said with a measure of fatherly pride. "The parents of that baby who was hospitalized after contracting RSV at Just Us Kids day care are looking into the possibility of filing a lawsuit. Your sister's investigating whether the day care center followed proper procedures or if that baby getting sick is a direct result of their negligence."

Realizing that he'd digressed, Ben changed direction. "She's set up her office down the hall and is already hunting for more clients," he told his son. "In the meantime, I'll make some calls about your options and get back to you with what I come up with."

Anderson was already heading out the door to see his sister. "Thanks, Dad."

"Thank me *after* I come up with something," Ben advised as he picked up his phone.

As he headed down the hall, Anderson discovered that Lindsay's door was open. Looking in, he saw that the inside of the small office looked as if it had been hit by a hurricane.

Hurricane Lindsay, he thought with a smile. Knocking on the door frame, Anderson walked in as his sister looked over her shoulder in his direction. "Dad said I should look in on you."

Lindsay froze. At twenty-five, the five-foot-five young woman with her long brown hair and penetrating blue eyes was the baby of the family. The position came with perks as well as with a stigma.

"What did I do now?" she questioned wearily.

Anderson shrugged. "Nothing that I know of," he told her honestly. "Dad thought that you might be able to help me."

She was no more enlightened than she'd been a minute ago. "Help you how?"

"Lexie took Jake back home yesterday." No matter how casual he tried to sound about it, saying the words still hurt.

Lindsay stopped putting leather-bound books on her bookshelves and immediately made her way over to her big brother. She threw her arms around him to embrace him in a heartfelt hug.

"Oh, Anderson, I'm so sorry," she said, releasing him and stepping back to look at him as she spoke. "I really liked the little guy."

"Yeah, me, too," Anderson said heavily. "He didn't want to go, Lindsay. Lexie practically dragged him out of the house."

Apparently unable to imagine something so heartless, Lindsay shook her head. "You have lousy taste in women, big brother."

"So I keep being told," Anderson responded with a sigh. And then, desperate, he got down to business. "That's not the point, Linds. I need help in getting custody of Jake."

Far more familiar with the prospect than her father, Lindsay shook her head.

"It's not going to be easy," she told her brother, then got down to the specifics he would be battling. "You're a single dad who works long hours on his ranch and has zero experience with kids," she told him, pointing out all the things that she knew Lexie's lawyer would ultimately cite.

"Lexie's a single mother," Anderson protested. From his point of view, they were both facing the same handicap.

"The key word here is not *single*," Lindsay pointed out, "but *mother*. I don't like it," she admitted, "but unless Lexie has done something really awful that can be held against her, the judge will be inclined to award custody to her if that's what she's asking for.

"But let me look into this," she told Anderson once she saw her brother's dejected expression. "Maybe I can come up with some last-ditch plan. Give me a little bit," she asked.

What choice did he have, Anderson thought. Shrugging, he said, "Sure."

What else could he do?

When Anderson heard the knock on his door later that day, his first thought was to pretend he wasn't home. He wasn't up to seeing anyone, or pretending that he felt like talking.

But then he thought that maybe it was either his father or Lindsay—or both—here to see him about a possible custody strategy. Doing his best to raise his spirits in order to be able to face company—even his family—he went to answer the door.

It occurred to him just a beat before he opened the door that his father or Lindsay were far more likely to call than to just show up on the doorstep even though this was the family ranch, but by then it was too late. He was already opening the door.

And looking at Marina.

He did *not* feel like talking to the woman. Being polite, much less friendly, required far more effort than he had to give.

"If you're here to find out why Jake wasn't in school today, you're too late," he informed her coldly. "He's gone. His mother took him home to Chicago."

She was here for another reason, but Anderson's statement caught her off guard. Her heart ached for the boy. How could the woman have just dragged him away like that?

"I thought she wasn't supposed to be doing that until the weekend."

"Yeah, we all thought that," Anderson responded, making no effort to hide his bitterness. "But apparently she had other ideas. So, if there's nothing else," he began, ready to close the door again.

But Marina deftly slipped across the threshold and into his living room. Turning to look at him, she observed, "You look awful."

He didn't need to be told that, he knew. "Not exactly my finest hour," he told her crisply, then added in a voice that sounded far more forlorn, "I feel like a fool."

"Because she took him from you?" Marina questioned. That didn't make any sense to her. Jake's mother coming to take the boy back to Chicago with her certainly wasn't Anderson's fault.

"Because I actually thought she'd had a change of heart," he corrected. "Turns out she just needed someplace to dump Jake while she went off with her new lover. But apparently that relationship went sour pretty quickly—like so many of her *other* relationships—so she wanted Jake back. And she got him," he concluded with no small bitterness.

"Just like that?" Marina questioned. It took her breath away to think about it. Didn't the woman have any decency? She was traumatizing her own son. "How could she be so insensitive not to see that Jake was actually beginning to adjust to living here? To being *happy* here?" Marina protested.

Bitterness curved the corners of Anderson's mouth downward. "Lexie only sees what she wants to see. The rest she just blocks out at will," he recalled.

"That certainly doesn't sound like she'd be a candidate for the world's greatest mother," Marina told him. There was only one important point here. "You have to get Jake back."

Helpless, Anderson shrugged. *Tell me something I don't know*, he thought darkly.

Out loud he told her, "I don't know what else I can do. Supposedly, I have visitation rights. But if I try to get custody of Jake away from her, Lexie is threatening to revoke those visitation rights and I'll be back to where I was a year ago. Nowhere," he underscored angrily.

"Besides," he told her, already resigned to his fate—and hating it, "it wouldn't be fair keeping Jake away from his mother just because I have an ax to grind with the woman."

Was he serious? Jake's mother sounded like she was some kind of a monster. Jake would do well to be rid of her. But Marina knew she couldn't come out and say that, at least not yet.

"Why don't you try to get joint custody?" she wanted to know. To her, that was the first thing she would have thought of.

"My father and sister are already looking into it for me, but to be honest, I really doubt anything will come of that. Let's face it, with my background, if Lexie fights me on this, the court will side with her and, like I said, if she gets angry enough, she'll pull the rug right out from under me and I won't be able to see Jake at all. This is a case of something being better than nothing," he told her, resigned.

Marina thought for a moment, debating saying what was on her mind out loud. Then she decided to go for it. A boy's happiness was at stake.

Choosing her words carefully, she instantly piqued Anderson's attention when she asked him, "What if, when you applied for joint custody of your son, your situation changed?"

Chapter 15

Anderson looked at his son's teacher, confusion, not to mention frustration over the situation he found himself in, claiming his ability to think straight.

"Exactly what do you mean by 'changed'?" he wanted to know.

Marina spoke slowly, weighing each word as she attempted to decide if what she was about to suggest to Anderson would be welcomed—or rejected—by him. "Well, according to what you just said, it sounds like your chances of getting at least joint custody would be much better if the judge thought that you were a family man."

By some people's definition, just having Jake made him a family man. But he had a feeling that Marina wasn't talking about that.

"And by family man you mean...?"

Anderson still wasn't getting it because he was certain that she couldn't possibly be saying what he thought she was saying.

"I mean the usual thing," Marina replied. She was going to have to spell it out for him, wasn't she? *Okay,* she thought, resigned, *here goes nothing.* She hit the ground running. "A two-parent household with a schoolteacher mom—"

Maybe it shouldn't have, but the description hit him with the force of a two-by-four. He was stunned to say the least.

"Meaning you?"

"Meaning me," she confirmed almost as an aside, and then continued laying out the scenario. "It would certainly hold some sway with a judge and give you the leverage you need to be able to get cust—"

"Wait," he ordered, still looking at her in complete disbelief. "Are you *actually* saying that you would be willing to make this sacrifice for Jake? That you'd be willing to marry me so that I could get joint custody of my son?"

Yes, you idiot, that's what I'm saying. What did you think I was saying?

But she couldn't say the words out loud. She was afraid that Anderson would turn her down after she'd put herself on the line like this for him, or that he would accuse her of having some sort of ulterior motive. Instead, Marina asked him a question of her own.

"How would you feel about that?" She carefully watched his expression to gauge what Anderson was thinking.

"How would I feel?" Anderson echoed incredulously.

"Yes," she replied patiently, "That's what I just asked."

"How would I feel?" Anderson repeated again, stunned as well as overjoyed by the very magnitude of the sacrifice she was offering to make. "I'll show you how I feel," he cried.

Overwhelmed and thrilled by her offer and what it would ultimately mean for Jake, Anderson abruptly dropped his guard as well as his very controlled behavior. He literally grabbed Marina, pulled her to him and kissed her. Kissed her long and hard.

Kissed her with every fiber of the immense gratitude that throbbed within him.

"Lord, I don't know how to thank you," he cried, breathless.

Shaken down to her very core, Marina struggled to sound flippant and blasé rather than like someone who was very close to dissolving like hot candle wax.

"I think you just did," she heard herself murmur.

It was a complete mystery to Marina how she could remain standing upright when it felt as if her kneecaps had been completely melted away in the heat that was generated by Anderson's kiss.

And then, as she watched, she saw Anderson's expression sobering, going from pure joy to solemnity. Instantly, she felt her heart sinking.

"What's wrong?" she asked him.

All sorts of roadblocks were beginning to pop up in his head. "There's still the problem of the no-fraternizing rule at school," he told her.

Was that all? she thought, almost laughing out loud. "Well, that's easy enough to solve," she assured him.

The woman obviously had clearer insight into things than he had, Anderson thought. The tiniest spark of hope began to burn again even as he admitted, "I don't see how."

Anderson was too close to it, she thought. And too consumed with worry to see the actual picture. She did what she could to clear it up for him.

"If Jake's back in Chicago, then I'm not his teacher anymore. And if I'm not his teacher, then I'm not fraternizing with the parent of one of my students, am I?" she asked, spreading her hands as if to bring her point home. "Problem solved," she announced.

For her trouble, Marina found herself being hugged again. Hugged, and whirled around the room and then finally, kissed again.

Maybe it was just her imagination, but each time Anderson kissed her, his lips felt even more lethal to her than the last time. Now it wasn't just her knees but her whole body that felt like it was melting.

She was barely aware of putting her arms around his neck, but she needed to anchor herself to something while the foundation of her very world was rocked down to its bottom layer of concrete.

For the first time in his life, Anderson felt almost giddy. He told himself that the sensation rose out of relief, and not out of the fact that he was going to be marrying a woman who could, just by kissing him, make his mind go completely blank, even while the rest of him craved something far more substantial, far more basic than euphoria.

What she was doing just by kissing him was turning his very world upside down and making him forget every single one of the rules he had laid out for himself. Rules that had brought order to his life and to his very existence.

Those rules did not allow for him to even remotely entertain the idea of falling in love.

He blocked the thought from his mind and focused instead on the pragmatic side of what was happening.

Because of Marina's sacrifice, he was going to be able to have his son back in his life on a regular basis. He knew that he would always be eternally grateful to her for that.

And because he *was* trying to be pragmatic, he forced himself to examine everything, to leave nothing to last-minute upheavals.

"You're sure about this?" he questioned Marina. His eyes all but pinned her down intently. "About marrying me?"

"This would be a terrible time for me to shout, 'April Fools,'" she replied. Then, in case he was actually harboring any doubts, she quickly added, "Yes, I'm sure."

It should have satisfied him, he told himself—but it didn't. Because Lexie had turned on him so abruptly after their one night together, it had left a lasting impression on him. A very sour lasting impression. And that didn't begin to take into account the way she had kept his only son's very existence from him, then denied him any access to the boy once he did know about Jake.

It had made Anderson feel very leery and it caused him to be suspicious of everything. Especially something that seemed to be too good to be true. What if he was being set up for some reason? He couldn't abide something like that. Not again.

He looked at Marina. "What's in it for you?" he wanted to know.

Because her only thoughts were about Anderson and his son, his question completely threw her. "Excuse me?"

Impatience clawed at him. He hated how suspicious he'd become, but there was no getting away from it. His only recourse was to try to pin her down—and to hope she was as selfless as her actions painted her to be.

"Marrying me, giving up for your freedom so I can get custody of Jake, what's in it for you?" Anderson asked.

Obviously he didn't believe she was doing

this because she simply cared about the boy. She was going to have to convince him, Marina thought.

"You're not the only one who loves Jake," she said. "I'm doing this—offering to marry you—because Jake has every right to be happy. Because he's a terrific kid and I think he'd make a really good big brother for Sydney." She took a breath, knowing that she was crossing a line. But this had to be said. "And I'm doing it because, no offense, I think his mother is a witch and I'm afraid of how she might wind up warping his soul if she has sole custody of him.

"Jake is a good, decent, sweet kid who deserves to have a parent who puts his needs first, not a parent who sees him as an impediment to her next tryst." She stopped and looked at the expression on Anderson's face. She couldn't quite read it. *Had* she said too much? "What? Did I go too far?" she asked him.

Maybe he was still in love with Lexie despite everything the woman had done to him, Marina thought. Maybe he even resented her criticism of Jake's mother. In that case, she needed to backtrack—but she couldn't.

"I'm sorry," she apologized. "But that's what I think."

"Don't apologize," he told her, his voice stoic and completely unreadable.

"Okay," she said slowly, still feeling as if she was standing on ground that could, just like that, turn to quicksand. "But you still have this expression on your face that I can't quite make out. What are you thinking?" she forced herself to ask, feeling as if she really didn't have anything to lose at this point.

"What I'm thinking," he told her in very slow, deliberately measured out words, "is that I don't know how I got so lucky."

Marina blinked, certain that she had misheard him. It was just her desperate need to make him understand why she was ready to go through with this for him that had her putting words into Anderson's mouth.

"Excuse me?" she said in a soft voice.

"I said," he repeated, speaking louder, "I don't know how I got this lucky."

Somehow, his words were not penetrating her head. Maybe her own disbelief was preventing her from absorbing what he was telling her. She took a stab at clarifying things for herself. "You mean to get someone to marry you so that you could get custody of Jake."

Maybe she didn't want to put any more emphasis on what was actually happening between them than that, Anderson thought. Maybe admitting that there might be more going on than a simple convenient arrangement was too scary for her.

He could certainly identify with that, Anderson thought, what with the episode with Lexie looming in his past. He'd be willing to bet that Marina had gotten burned herself by the man who'd gotten her pregnant. For that matter, all she really knew about *him* was that he was Jake's father and that he desperately wanted custody of the boy.

Not exactly something to build forever on with a man, he thought. Especially when that man had suddenly and abruptly severed all ties with her after a month of some pretty good, not to mention intense weekends, he rationalized. Looking back, he realized that he could have handled that so much better than he had.

He needed to make amends for that, Anderson told himself.

He also told himself that right now, it would be for the best if he just went with the scenario that she had handed him. They were both going to do this—to marry one another—for Jake's sake, so that he could come back to Rust Creek Falls.

"Yeah," Anderson agreed. "What you said."

And then, because Marina made him feel so exuberantly happy, Anderson found himself kissing her again.

And again.

Because each time, it was better than the last and it made him want to sample the next time. And the next.

So, just for this very short interlude in time, he did.

Deepening the kiss, Anderson kissed her as if there was no tomorrow, no moments to follow this one. All there was, was now.

But it was enough.

"Last chance to change your mind," Anderson warned her several days later.

They were standing in a room that was right outside a judge's chambers in Kalispell. Instead of being in a church filled with her friends and her sister, Dawn, and Dawn's new husband, Marina would soon be facing a middle-aged man who had only a fringe of hair to call his own and a solemn air about him that made her think of her first elementary school principal, Mr. Oshinsky.

But those were just trappings, Marina reminded herself. Just the mere daydreams of an adolescent girl who was given to romanticizing things. They *weren't* what was really important here.

All that mattered was Jake—and of course Sydney, both of whom, with this one short act on her part, would be getting a kind, loving man as their father. Jake would be getting him because of course Anderson was his father, and Sydney would be getting him because both Jake and Anderson were crazy about her. They would make certain that her little girl would be getting a loving home out of this arrangement.

So, if she was sacrificing bells and whistles, as well as a misty dose of romance and all the things that went with it, well, she was a big girl, Marina told herself. The benefits to be gotten out of this union far outweighed what she was giving up.

"Marina?" Anderson softly prodded, obviously waiting for her response to his question.

Embarrassed to be caught mentally adrift this way, Marina flushed and apologized to him quickly. "I'm sorry, what?"

Anderson repeated his question, concerned that maybe she didn't answer because she *didn't* want to go through with this arrangement after all.

"I asked if you're sure about going through with this."

Marina raised her chin defensively. "Of course I'm sure. I wouldn't be here if I wasn't," she told him with conviction. "My only regret is that you couldn't get Jake to be here."

He didn't want to think about the conversation he'd had with Lexie just yesterday. The memory of the sound of her voice would be enough to put him in a bad mood and Marina deserved better than that for the sacrifice she was making for him.

All he would let himself say was, "Lexie's not convinced it's going to happen and she didn't want to allow Jake to fly out here until after she was sure we'd gone through with it."

That was one highly suspicious woman, Marina thought. Everything she'd heard about Lexie so far had her thoroughly disliking her.

"Didn't you tell her that you'd pay for the plane ticket?"

"I did." It was the first thing he'd said when he called her. The first thing Lexie had said to him was *No*. "But that didn't seem to make any difference to her."

"I was right," Marina concluded. "Jake's mother really *is* a witch. I'm glad we're saving him."

"We're not," Anderson corrected. When she started to question him, he told her, "You are."

She was pleased that he thought that, but she'd never been one to take credit as her due. "Not without you, I'm not."

Just then, the judge's legal intern peeked into the room where they were waiting. The hint of a smile was on her thin lips.

"Judge Wyatt is ready to marry you now," the young woman told them.

Anderson rose to his feet, then turned toward Marina and put his hand out to her. When she wrapped her fingers around it, he drew her up so that she was standing right beside him.

Marina could feel her heart pounding. Adrenaline was doing double-time in her veins. It was really happening, she thought.

"I guess this is it," Marina murmured.

Anderson nodded. "Showtime," he told her.

The judge's intern, Josephine Vickers, said, "This way, please," as she turned on her neatly stacked heel and led the way back into the judge's chambers.

Tucking Marina's arm through his, Anderson lowered his head to hers and apologized in a hushed whisper. "I'm sorry this isn't in a church." He sensed that she would have preferred the latter.

But if she was disappointed, Marina gave no indication. "We would have had to wait too long and every minute that goes by is another minute that Jake believes that he was abandoned by the people he thought loved him."

Anderson turned toward her before they crossed the threshold into the chambers. He wanted one more moment in private with Marina.

"You really are a very rare woman," he told her with admiration.

Marina smiled, her heart warmed by his praise more than she could possibly begin to tell him. Instead, she turned to humor.

"I'm a fifth-grade teacher," she told him. "It comes with the territory."

The judge looked somewhat impatient as they entered his chambers. It was obvious that he had somewhere else to be.

"Mr. Dalton, Ms. Laramie," he said, greeting them each in turn with a nod. "I'm Judge Wyatt and I'm pressed for time, so shall we get on with it?" he asked, looking from one to the other.

He really wasn't asking a question; he was putting them on notice.

Some very short notice, it turned out, because as he began to officiate the service, his rather monotone cadence seemed to speed up and he said all the words of the ceremony so quickly, they barely had time to register before he uttered the final ones.

"And I now pronounce you husband and wife. Thank you and good luck!"

And just like that, they were married.

Chapter 16

He was grateful to Marina, he really was. Because of her, he felt that he at least had a shot at getting his son back in his life, if only on a part-time basis.

She deserved something better than a quickie wedding ceremony in a brusque judge's chambers, even if this wasn't a real love match.

Feeling slightly sheepish, Anderson looked at her as they walked down the steps of the courthouse less than half an hour after they had entered the building. "Not exactly the wedding of your dreams, was it?" he asked Marina.

She wasn't going to dwell on what it wasn't,

only on what it was. "It got the job done," she told him brightly.

"That's not what I asked you," Anderson pointed out tactfully.

He appreciated the fact that she didn't carry on about how lacking the ceremony was. In her place, he knew Lexie would have gone on about it for hours, possibly days. But that still didn't make the actual occurrence any better.

Standing at the bottom step, Marina was forced to admit, "I doubt that any woman dreams of standing in front of a frowning, balding man in a suit with a soup stain just above his breast pocket, listening to him say the words that are meant to bind her forever to someone in the eyes of the law."

He laughed shortly as he shook his head. "Very pragmatically stated. Soup stain, huh?" On top of everything else, the woman was incredibly observant, he thought.

She nodded. "Just above his breast pocket," she repeated. "A faint one." And then she shrugged philosophically. "Like I said, it got the job done. In the eyes of the law, I am your wife and we are a unit." She began to walk over to his truck. "A family. I've got a very good record as a teacher, you're a good, hardworking man." Marina got into the vehicle on her side, then closed the door. She waited until he got in on his side before continuing. "There is no reason in the world why you wouldn't be granted at least partial custody of Jake," she told him, buckling up.

Anderson paused, listening to the woman he had just made his wife. They had just gotten married for very practical reasons. This was supposed to be more of a covenant, an agreement, than anything else, and yet, he could swear that because of what she said and her gracious behavior in a less than ideal situation, he could feel himself falling in love with her. Falling in love with her selflessness, with the way he'd observed her acting around Jake.

She wasn't just a good teacher, she was a born mother. And there was no denying the fact that he was attracted to her. When he kissed her—well, all he knew was that he'd never known two friends to kiss this way. As the old expression went, she certainly lit his fire. And yet, all the while, all she seemed to think about or focus on were Jake's and Sydney's needs, not her own.

For that matter, she was putting him before herself, as well. It was as if she didn't count in this grand scheme of things.

He had never met anyone quite like Marina.

"Tell me, how would you feel about going on a honeymoon?" he asked her out of the blue.

Her hand froze midway in securing her seat belt. It took her a couple of seconds to absorb what he was asking her. Her mind had been going in an entirely different direction.

Marina blinked as she looked at him incredulously. "A what?"

"A honeymoon," he repeated, amused at the bewildered expression on her face. She looked almost adorable. "You know, what a couple goes on after they get married."

She couldn't tell if he was just pulling her leg, or if he was actually serious. How was she going to train herself not to have any feelings for this man if he kept derailing her like this? If he kept throwing out thoughts that teased her and caused havoc with the mind-set she was trying so hard to assume? She would have loved to go on a honeymoon, but that wasn't what all this was supposed to be about.

"Conventional people," Marina pointed out. "The kind who are focused on each other and just having fun, not gearing up to do battle over custody issues with the Wicked Witch of the West. Besides," she gently reminded him, "Sydney is still an infant. I can't leave her for a week, much less two," she protested, then, after a moment, she added in a much quieter voice, "No matter how nice the idea of a honeymoon might seem."

The selfless practicality of the woman astounded him. "All right, then how about an overnight stay at Maverick Manor?" he suggested, not ready to just give up on the idea of doing *something* to show Marina how grateful he was. "I know someone there who can get us a very nice suite." He put his key into the ignition, but still held off starting his truck. Instead, he looked at Marina. "It doesn't seem right for a couple to get married and then just plunge back into their daily lives without at least *some* sort of an acknowledgment that something different has happened.

"Unless, of course, you don't want to," he suddenly qualified, realizing that maybe Marina didn't want any more attention brought to the fact that they were married.

If you only knew how much I want to go on that honeymoon, Marina thought. *You'd be knocked right out of your boots.*

"Why wouldn't I want to?" she questioned out loud, curious as to his thought process.

He didn't have a gift with words, he never had. That was why he preferred being a rancher and hadn't followed his father into a career as a lawyer. The fact of the matter was he didn't really know how to express himself, but he knew he had to give it a try.

"I thought that maybe you'd want as little attention called to our, um, 'arrangement' as possible," he finally said.

Her eyebrows drew together as she tried to find a reason why he would think this way. Try as she might, she came up empty. "Isn't that the whole point of this? To call attention to the fact that we're married and can create a good home for Jake?"

She had him there. "I guess you're right." He thought for a moment, then went back to his last proposal. "So, since you can't be away from Sydney for any great length of time, why don't we do what I suggested and just go for an overnight stay at the hotel?" he asked, watching her face to see how she really felt about the matter. "Would that be all right?"

Marina really wished she could gauge how *he* felt about the idea of a honeymoon. But, since she couldn't, she felt she could at least tell him what she thought of his suggestion.

"That would be perfect." She did her best to try to curb her enthusiasm. She didn't want to scare him away. "I can get Dawn to baby-sit Sydney overnight. She's already told me that she would be more than willing to take the baby for a night when I dropped her off earlier today."

Or two, Marina silently added, recalling her younger sister's words. She had a feeling that Dawn was trying to see what kind of a parent she'd make before taking the plunge and becoming pregnant herself.

"Then it's settled," Anderson said, pleased. "I'll give my friend at Maverick Manor a call and as long as your sister's available for the job, we can leave right after school's over tomorrow—sooner if you want to take the day off," he added.

She did, but she didn't feel that it was right. "I already took today off. I don't want the kids to think I've abandoned them."

Absolutely incredible, he couldn't help thinking. *The woman's a saint.*

"Fair enough," he told her out loud, finally starting the truck. "I'll come by tomorrow and pick you up from school, Mrs. Dalton," Anderson added after a beat, then realized that, again, he'd wound up taking something for granted. "Unless, of course, you want to continue being called Ms. Laramie."

But Marina shook her head. She loved the idea of taking his name, but again, she didn't want to scare him off so instead she said, "That might confuse everyone."

Anderson was more than happy to accommodate her. "Mrs. Dalton it is."

He had to admit, he liked the sound of that.

She might not have had a dream wedding. But in all the fantasies that she did have about the man she might someday marry, the husband she envisioned definitely paled in comparison to the man who walked into her classroom the following afternoon.

Anderson Dalton, at six foot one, with his slightly shaggy light brown hair and his electric blue eyes was just the kind of stuff that fantasies were made of. She felt her pulse skip a beat when she looked up and saw him standing there in her doorway.

"Ready?" he asked, his deep voice rumbling and filling up all the space around her.

"Ready," she echoed, closing the middle drawer of her desk and locking it. "I just have to grab my suitcase. I packed a few things," she explained. "If that's all right."

"Sure it's all right." Why would she even doubt that? he wondered. "I'm not kidnapping you, we're going on a honeymoon. An abbreviated one," he qualified, "but still a honeymoon. I didn't assume you wanted to rough it—any more than you already are," he added with what sounded like an apologetic note.

She was nervous, but his apologetic tone put her a little more at ease.

"Let's go, then," she said, picking up her suitcase from behind her desk.

"Let's," Anderson echoed as he took the suitcase from her and walked behind her out of the classroom.

Her nerves were back, growing progressively more pronounced the closer they came to the hotel. By the time she found herself standing before the honeymoon suite, her nerves had grown to towering proportions.

Opening the doors for them, the hotel attendant smiled politely and then silently withdrew, leaving them alone in the suite.

Anderson couldn't remember the last time he had felt nervous, but for some reason, he realized that he was nervous as he waited for her reaction. Pleasing Marina had suddenly become important to him.

"Do you like it?" he asked, intently watching her face.

"It's big," Marina acknowledged. It seemed like a safe thing to say. Looking around, it all began to sink in for her. This was real. She was married to Anderson Dalton and standing in the honeymoon suite—and she hadn't a clue how to act. Did she let him realize that she loved him? Or did she do her very best to act as if she was just going through the motions?

She continued talking about the suite because it felt safe.

"I think it's bigger than my apartment." She moved around the room, gauging the size. "You could have a party in here," she told him. Her nerves were practically strangling her.

"A party for two," Anderson replied. Realizing that sounded as if he was putting pressure on her, he immediately attempted to do damage control. "I mean, if that's what someone wanted to do. It is, after all, a honeymoon suite."

This wasn't coming out right. He cleared his throat and tried again, wanting to make sure that Marina didn't feel that he was thinking of taking advantage of her because they were legally married now. "The suite has two rooms."

She looked at him, thinking that sounded rather odd. "A honeymoon suite with two rooms? Isn't that strange?" She'd only been in a hotel room once, and it had been a tiny thing. Even so, there had been two beds shoved into it. Hardly room for a person to walk, she re-called. Here, they could have installed a bowl-ing alley if they'd been so inclined.

"One's a bedroom," he told her, feeling more awkward by the moment, "the other is where they can share a private meal if they want to. It's got a couch so I can sleep on that if—" The knock on the door interrupted him, bringing with it a wave of relief. "That's got to be room service," he told her.

"Room service?" she repeated. "Did we order room service?" She didn't recall either one of them doing so. They'd just walked in. There had to be some sort of a mistake.

"Yes, we did," Anderson assured her as he went to the door. "I thought that a little pri-vacy might be nice. But we can eat down in the restaurant if you'd rather do that," he told her, wanting to stay entirely flexible for her.

"Room service is fine," she told him, doing her best not to let her nerves get the better of her. It wasn't easy.

Room service was more than fine, it was ex-quisite. She couldn't remember ever having a meal as sumptuous as the one Anderson had ordered for them.

The man might look like a cowboy, she

thought, but somewhere in that broad chest beat the heart of a man with sophisticated tastes.

Along with the filet mignon and the lobster tail came a bottle of champagne that seemed to heighten all her senses and make her acutely aware of just how much the man sitting across from her at their small table for two actually aroused her.

By the time they had gotten to dessert—a chocolate parfait—she felt as if the temperature in the room had gone up more than ten degrees—and was getting steadily warmer.

"I had no idea you could eat so much," Anderson said as the last bite of parfait disappeared behind her lips. He was extremely pleased that she'd enjoyed the meal he had ordered for them.

"Neither did I," she laughed.

"I can order more," he offered. "Maybe another dessert?"

"Oh please, I couldn't take another bite, not without possibly exploding," she confessed. And then she smiled at him. "This was all just perfect."

No, she was perfect. The meal was just good, Anderson thought.

Putting down his napkin, he glanced at his

watch. He hadn't realized it was so late. Talking with Marina, time had just managed to escape him.

He pushed the table aside and rose to his feet. "It's getting late and you're probably tired. I should let you get to bed."

Marina was immediately up. "Where are you going to sleep?" she asked.

She was testing him, wasn't she? Anderson thought. "Well, like I said, there's a couch here."

She looked at it. It was a lovely piece of furniture, but it was curved. Definitely not the sort of thing a person over the age of nine could sleep on.

"That can't be comfortable," she told him. "There's hardly enough room to stretch out."

His mind hadn't really been focused on the sofa. Now that he looked at it, she was right. "There's always the floor," he pointed out.

But she shook her head. "Even more uncomfortable," she told him. "There's a king-size bed in the other room," Marina reminded him. "It's certainly big enough for two people."

The idea of sharing a bed with her was far too tempting—resisting her now was already hard enough for him.

"I'm not so sure about that."

She looked at him for a long moment. She supposed what she said next she could have blamed on the champagne, but that would have been a lie. Because she'd thought about one thing ever since she had agreed to marry him.

"I am," she told Anderson quietly.

He could feel his heart quickening, but for her sake, if not his own, he had to talk some sense into her. "You don't know what you're saying, Marina."

She was already threading her arms around his neck, already bringing her body up against him, standing so close that a whisper wouldn't have been able to get through.

"I think I am," she told him, her voice low.

Did she realize how hard she was making this for him? "Marina, I'm only human. You keep standing so close to me like this and I'm not going to be able to do the right thing."

"I think you're doing the right thing right now," she told him, her warm breath gliding seductively along his neck and his skin. Cocking her head ever so slightly, she looked up into his eyes. "I'm your wife, Anderson," she whispered.

"I know that." If this was some sort of a test, he was failing it, he thought, feeling himself slipping. "That's what the wedding certificate says."

Her eyes never left his and he could feel himself getting lost in them. "I want to be your wife in every sense of the word, not just on paper."

This was a great deal more difficult than he had ever imagined. No, scratch that. It was beyond difficult. It was next to impossible and getting more so by the second.

"Oh damn it, Marina, I can't keep holding you at arm's length—"

"Then don't," she urged, rising up on her toes and kissing him.

She felt it instantly, felt him giving in to her, surrendering. Felt the kiss deepening and with it, the charade that they were both pretending to take part in ceased to exist.

Felt him wanting her.

Wanting her just as much as she wanted him.

She could feel a small whoop of joy echoing within her as her anticipation increased tenfold.

Their marriage was about to officially begin.

Chapter 17

Marina admittedly had never been very experienced when it came to having sex. To her, the idea of doing it if love wasn't involved was completely off-putting, so her partners over the years had been less than a handful. Moreover, it had been over a year since she had even felt a man's touch. Since her affair with Gary had ended so badly she hadn't even been tempted to make love with anyone. It was a complication she wanted no part of.

She thought—assumed—that she was just fine on her own. She actually felt content in the fact that it was just her and Sydney against the world. There was no need for her to yearn for a man in her life.

And yet, right at this moment, she couldn't think of anything she wanted more than to make love with Anderson, than to have him touch her, kiss her, possess her and make her his in every exquisite sense of the word.

Marina gave herself up to the sensation and sealed herself to her destiny—and Anderson.

She didn't remember just how or when their clothes had come off, didn't remember how they had gotten from the one room to the bedroom, much less into the king-size bed that dominated the room.

All she was aware of was this burning need to love and be wanted, to be taken up beyond the boundaries of the mortal world and into a realm where there were only two individuals who made up the population.

Anderson and her.

"Am I going too fast?" he'd asked her at one point, just before they'd landed on the bed.

"Your timing is perfect," she'd managed to get out. She found that she had to concentrate in order to get her breathing under control.

It was all he needed to hear to inflame him and urge him on to higher plateaus.

That was when it actually hit him, that it

all became crystal clear to him: he didn't ever want to let Marina go. Not because she was helping him get Jake back—that was part of it, but it wasn't the main part. He didn't want to let her go because he was in love with her. In love with a beautiful, pure woman who wanted nothing from him, nothing but to help him.

How could he have possibly gotten so lucky?

He wanted to tell Marina how he felt, to shout about the glorious feelings going on inside him from the highest rooftops. But he was afraid that if he let her suspect how he felt, it might just ultimately frighten her away. So all he could do was *show* her. And he intended to, for as long as she would let him.

He made love to her with a vengeance.

Something had changed.

Marina could feel it. Or maybe it was just the champagne that was finally kicking into high gear.

Whatever was at the root of it, she could have sworn that Anderson's lovemaking had escalated another notch—maybe even several. His lips were everywhere, making her crazy, branding her, causing her very skin to feel as if it was on fire. And the hotter it felt, the more she burned for him.

Her head was spinning and a stray little voice within her was whispering, *This is special, this is something unique. This is definitely a man who could easily rock my world.*

What "could"? she mocked herself. There was no doubt that he already was doing just that.

It suddenly occurred to her that she didn't want him coming away thinking she was only there to take from him. She needed to let him see that she was just as capable of giving back.

So she did.

Somewhere deep inside her, something very basic rose to the surface. It was bent on pleasing Anderson, on making him not regret this marriage of convenience they had struck up.

She wanted to make Anderson want her every bit as much as she wanted him.

Marina found herself acting on instincts she never even knew she possessed. Instincts Anderson had, just by making love with her, by arousing her with his skillful foreplay, brought out of her.

And just like that, she was giving him just as much pleasure as he had been giving her. Hearing Anderson moan acted like a catalyst and ignited her.

Marina had no idea where any of this came

from, she only knew that suddenly, she had skills that had never been there before, fueled by urges that had never existed before.

Empowered, exhilarated, she reacted to it all as if it was perfectly natural for her to do so.

Anderson had had no idea, when he had walked in on his son's teacher that first afternoon in her classroom, that beneath this woman's cool, classic exterior resided the soul of a tigress.

His own personal tigress.

Foreplay lasted longer than he ever thought himself capable of maintaining. He pleasured Marina for as long as he could hold out, until his self-control was about to break apart. He needed to join with her *now*!

Rolling over so that Marina was beneath him, Anderson primed her with openmouthed kisses all along her smooth, writhing body until neither of them could hold back even a fraction of a second longer.

His heart pounding wildly in his chest, Anderson entered her, making them one unit— for now and for always.

Tapping into what he knew was his last drop of self-control, Anderson began to move slowly.

And then faster.

And faster still, until he thought the tempo they reached was as close to the speed of light as humanly possible. And they were doing it together. That was all that seemed to matter, that they were arriving at the very peak of the mountain they were scaling together.

Standing at the top of the world together.

And then the very final thrust came, bringing all the stars raining down around them.

He clung to her, amazed at how hard his heart was beating without breaking through his ribs and shattering his chest wall.

He was even more amazed at how much he wanted her—again. Wanted her with every fiber of his being even though there wasn't a single ounce of energy left within him.

Marina reveled in the incredible magnitude of the feeling she'd just experienced, reveled in the fact that he was still holding her as if she was the most precious part of his world rather than just rolling away from her because he was done.

She could feel his heart mimicking her own and she had a surprising reaction to that.

A feeling of safety.

She'd never felt so safe, so secure in her entire life, not even when she'd been a child. Marina thought that she was probably reading things into this moment, but for now, she was content just to enjoy the sensation. To enjoy the feeling of his arms around her. To enjoy the calming pretense that she was Anderson's wife and that Anderson was her husband.

To enjoy the pretense that she was one half of a couple.

Reality would be on her doorstep all too soon, but not now. Not yet.

Marina resisted waking up.

The dream she was having, had been having, was too strong, too good to release. She wanted to hang on a little longer, cling to it and pretend that it was real for just a few more moments.

But something nudged at her consciousness, reminding Marina that the rest of her life was waiting for her. With a reluctant sigh, she opened her eyes—and saw that Anderson was lying next to her, propped up on his elbow and watching her.

"What are you doing?" she asked self-consciously. Was he regretting marrying her already? Had another plan occurred to him, one in which he didn't need her to play the role of his wife? Had he realized how disappointing she was in bed?

These and so many other thoughts assailed her as she struggled to get her bearings.

"I'm watching you sleep. And now," he continued with a smile she found infinitely sexy even with her nerves vibrating at top speed, "I'm watching you wake up."

Maybe it was going to be all right? It struck her as a question rather than a statement. "Are you that bored?" she asked hesitantly.

"I'm not bored at all," Anderson told her, allowing his fingers to slowly trail along the hollow of her throat. Arousing himself, arousing her. "Not by a long shot." His lips slowly made their way to the other side of her neck. "Last night was eye-opening," he whispered softly, his breath arousing her further.

She was having a very difficult time just lying there, having him doing what he was doing without responding. She didn't want him thinking that she demanded anything from him in any way.

"How so?" she breathed.

His voice was low and incredibly seductive. "I had no idea you were so talented, so skilled in so many different ways."

"You're laughing at me," Marina said, struggling to keep her eyes from shutting, to keep herself from drifting away.

"I might want to do many things with you, Marina, but laughing at you is definitely not one of them," he told her.

She was trembling again. Maybe she hadn't disappointed him last night and what had happened between them wasn't an isolated occurrence.

Her heart was hammering hard as she whispered, "What kind of things?"

"I'm a man of few words, Marina. I'm a lot better at showing what I mean rather than saying what I mean," he said.

Her pulse was practically beating right out of her body as she whispered, "Well, then I guess you'd better show me."

His smile went straight to her inner core as he said, "I thought you'd never ask."

Marina felt as if she had somehow unwittingly stumbled into a dreamworld. For one week, one wondrous week, absolutely everything was perfect. She didn't think it was humanly possible to be happier.

She moved in with Anderson, went to work every day to teach her students and came home each night to her little family. A family that she had every hope would be increased by one very soon.

Even Sydney, who had always been such an easy baby, seemed somehow happier than usual. And Lindsay had found them a lawyer who was certain that with everything that was going on, winning partial custody of Jake was all but a done deal.

And then on the afternoon of the eighth day, everything changed.

Marina drove up in her car to see another, unfamiliar vehicle parked right in front of the ranch house. Seeing it brought along a sense of vague uneasiness. She was familiar with all the cars and trucks that the members of Anderson's family drove and this vehicle didn't belong to any of them.

It could just belong to one of Anderson's friends, someone she wasn't acquainted with, but for some reason, she didn't believe that. Instead, all sorts of bells and alarms insisted on going off in her head.

Something was wrong.

She could feel it in her bones.

Part of Marina wanted to turn around and drive right back to school, to find some paperwork she'd forgotten about and needed to finish—except that she knew that there wasn't any. She was, among other things, conscientiousness personified. Her reports were always in ahead of time and never just under the wire, much less forgotten about.

Besides, if there *was* something going on, she needed to face it. Running away didn't make it disappear; it just prolonged the inevitable moment when she had to face whatever it was that was happening.

It was probably nothing.

It didn't *feel* like nothing.

The argument in her head went on for a prolonged moment, and then Marina forced herself to walk into the house.

Rather than enter and brightly announce, "I'm home," the way she had been doing for the past week, Marina quietly let herself into the house, all but tiptoeing in. Not because she wanted to catch Anderson doing something he shouldn't, but because if there was something going on she needed to be prepared for, having a moment to observe what that something was might be helpful.

The next moment, as she soundlessly approached the living room, she could hear two people talking. And just like that, she could feel her soul shrinking back not in fear, but in total distress.

One of the voices belonged to Anderson, the other to some woman.

A woman whose identity quickly made itself known by what she was saying.

The other woman was Lexie, Jake's mother. And Anderson's former lover.

The thought throbbed over and over in her head: Lexie was standing in the living room.

In *her* living room.

If her heart had sunk down any farther, it would have gone straight through the floor.

Rather than step forward, Marina remained frozen in the shadows, listening to what they were saying. It quickly became apparent that the woman had gotten here only a couple of minutes ago.

And Lexie did not sound as if she was leaving.

The next second, Marina realized that the woman had brought Jake back with her. Maybe this wasn't as bad as she'd thought. Maybe things were finally falling into place.

But the knot in her stomach didn't think so.

"Jake," Lexie said, "why don't you go to your room? I want to talk to your dad."

Anderson knew his son, having just gotten here, was reluctant to go anywhere. He wanted to stay near his father. "Can't I stay with you, Dad?" he pleaded.

"You *are* staying with him, Jake," Lexie told

her son impatiently. "Now listen to me and go to your room," she said. Her voice softened the next moment as she added, "Just for now."

"Do as she says, Jake," Anderson told his son, releasing the boy after he'd hugged him. "We'll talk in a few minutes," he promised.

"Okay." Jake reluctantly obeyed and shuffled out of the room and then up the stairs.

"All right, Lexie, you've gotten the boy out of the room. Now what's this big thing you want to say to me that you can't say in front of Jake?" Anderson wanted to know.

There was a long pause, as if Lexie was searching for the right words—or her courage. "I wanted to apologize," she finally told him stiffly.

"For?" Anderson asked, somehow managing to hide his surprise.

This was obviously hard for her, but Anderson wasn't about to make it any easier. He stood there in silence, waiting for her to go on.

"For using you," Lexie finally said.

"You're going to have to be more specific than that," he told her gruffly. "What you just apologized for wasn't a onetime deal."

"When we…had that one night together," Lexie began, struggling with each word, "I was seeing someone else at the time."

Over time, Anderson had assumed as much. "Go on," he instructed.

She closed her eyes for a moment, searching for words. "When I realized I was pregnant, I panicked. I figured I could pass the baby off to my boyfriend as his. For a while, he wasn't the wiser and I really didn't think you'd care one way or the other—after all, it was just a fling between us," she reminded Anderson. "Anyway, my boyfriend and I got married and for a while, everything was good." Her expression became more somber. "But it didn't last. To be honest, I don't think that Jake remembers him at all."

She took a breath, then continued. "I guess what I'm actually apologizing for is keeping Jake and you apart all this time. A boy needs his father. I can see that now. Ever since I brought Jake back home with me, he's been completely withdrawn and sullen. I realized that it's because he misses you so much."

"So you've decided to give me partial custody?" Anderson asked hopefully. He couldn't see this heading in any other direction, but he took nothing for granted when it came to Lexie.

"Better than that," Lexie told him, smiling broadly for the first time and obviously very pleased with herself.

"Go on," he urged when she paused to bask in what she was about to tell him.

"I wanted you to know that I'm making a fresh start, Anderson. I've decided to move here to Montana so that you and Jake can see each other on a regular basis."

The cry of dismay escaped Marina's voice before she could stop it.

Chapter 18

Hearing the stifled cry, Anderson immediately left Lexie and went around the corner that separated the living room from the foyer. He was surprised to find Marina standing there.

"Marina, when did you get home?" he asked, puzzled why she hadn't just come in when she heard him talking to Lexie.

Marina was trying her very best not to look flustered. She would have loved to have just disappeared into the woodwork, and silently upbraided herself for calling attention to herself this way.

"Just now," she answered, hoping she didn't

look as upset as she felt, especially when Lexie stepped into the foyer.

What she had just overheard had knocked the very air out of her lungs. She felt numb. If Lexie was moving here to Montana, to live somewhere close to Anderson so that Jake could interact with his father, then there was no need for Anderson to remain married to her. Just like that, she had outlived her usefulness.

"Ms. Laramie?"

All three adults turned at the sound of the high-pitched, elated cry. Jake came flying down the stairs and went straight to Marina.

"I thought I heard your voice!" he cried happily, throwing his arms around her waist and hugging her as hard as he could.

Lexie looked completely put out by her son's obvious display of affection.

"Jake, I thought we told you to stay in your room," she said, clearly annoyed that Jake had disobeyed her. "See what I mean?" she asked, turning toward Anderson. "He doesn't listen to me anymore. He *always* listened to me before he came out here," Lexie lamented.

"Maybe you're mistaking listening for just not hearing you," Anderson tactfully pointed out, much to the other woman's obvious displeasure. "When he first came here, he was completely consumed with video games. Someone could have told him he was on fire and he wouldn't have paid any attention. It was Marina who turned him around, who got him to pay attention and to study. She saw the lonely kid that neither one of us realized was there and found a way to reach him."

Marina, still hugging Jake, looked at Anderson, utterly stunned and totally pleased. She had no idea that any of this had actually registered with Jake's father. She had just assumed that Anderson thought his son had come around on his own. She certainly wouldn't have pointed it out to him. She had never been out for any credit; she only wanted the boy to be happy. The sadness in his eyes had made her determined to turn him around.

For her part, Lexie looked completely surprised at the revelation.

"Is this true?" she asked. Her question was open-ended. As it stood, it could have been intended for either her son or for Marina.

It was Jake who replied. He looked up at his mother, answering her question almost shyly.

"Ms. Laramie talks to me. She makes me feel good about myself, like just because I didn't know what all the other kids knew didn't mean that I couldn't learn."

Lexie looked taken aback and somewhat humbled. "Is this true?" she asked, looking at Marina.

Marina was at a loss as to how to answer. She really didn't want to sound as if she was bragging, or trying to come between either Jake and his mother, or Anderson and Jake's mother. But she didn't want to lie, either.

She settled for something simple and vague. "Every child just needs a little guidance to help access his or her full potential. That's my job as a teacher," Marina said.

Lexie's expression softened somewhat. She even smiled a little.

"So I guess I did a good thing by bringing Jake here," Lexie said. "Thanks," she told Marina and then turned toward Anderson. "I was thinking of leaving Jake here with you so he can enroll back in school while I go back to Chicago and make all the necessary arrangements to move our things out here."

Suddenly Marina felt as if she was intruding on family business. "Why don't I just go see about getting dinner ready while you two talk logistics."

Jake popped up in front of her. "Can I help?" he asked her eagerly.

Marina thought that Jake was probably better off staying with his parents, but he looked so enthusiastic, she didn't have the heart to turn him down.

"Of course you can," she told Jake fondly, putting her arm around the boy's shoulders. "Have you seen Sydney yet? I know that she'll be so happy to see you," Marina told him as they walked into the kitchen.

Jake looked surprised by the news. "Sydney's here in the house?" he asked happily. "Where?"

The playpen had been empty when she'd entered the living room. "Well, since I didn't see her when I walked in, I guess your dad probably put her down for another nap in her room."

"Sydney has her own room here?" Jake asked her, surprised and clearly excited by the news.

That was when she realized that Anderson probably hadn't told his son that they were married. She was tempted to tell him herself, but that would have been selfish of her, done for ulterior motives. This wasn't her story to tell.

Besides, maybe Anderson didn't want to tell Jake that they had gotten married. There was no longer a need for that charade to continue and maybe it was just easier for him not to say anything at all about it. That way, the boy wouldn't get confused, she reasoned, doing her very best to be objective about the situation rather than emotional. But it was hard to deny the way she really felt.

Jake, she realized, was still waiting for her to explain why Sydney had her own room here. "It's easier when she goes down for a nap to put her somewhere that she won't be disturbed," Marina explained.

"Oh." The excuse seemed to satisfy him. "Want me to set the table?" he volunteered brightly.

She was throwing together pulled chicken, which she had already prepared the night before, along with several vegetables that just needed to be steamed. All that was really left to be done was to mix everything together in a big pot on the stove and warm it up. That wouldn't take very long.

She gave Jake an encouraging smile. "That would be very helpful."

The moment Jake left the room, his arms loaded down with dinner plates, Marina felt her eyes beginning to sting.

She wasn't going to cry, she told herself. She was going to hold it together for Jake's sake and then, after dinner, she would collect her daughter and go back to her apartment. She'd given her notice to the landlord at the beginning of the week, but if she appealed to the man's better nature, he might allow her to rescind it. That meant that she could just go back to living in the apartment.

And, with any luck, she could get her life back on track in about a dozen years or so, she thought as a tear spilled out.

Damn it, she wasn't going to go to pieces. She wasn't, she told herself sternly. The last thing she wanted was for Anderson to feel sorry for her—or to have him be shamed into letting her remain on the ranch.

For all she knew, now that Lexie was back, maybe he would even pick up their relationship where it had dropped off twelve years ago. Stranger things had been known to happen. After all, they did have a child together.

Marina heard a noise behind her. Jake was back for the rest of the dinnerware, she thought. The boy moved fast.

"Don't forget, knives on the right, forks on the left," she told him automatically. She kept her back to him, not wanting Jake to see her cry. There would be endless questions if he did.

An amused voice asked, "And where do the spoons go?"

Caught off guard, Marina dropped the spatula she was using to stir the pulled chicken. She whirled around to face Anderson.

"Sorry," she apologized, immediately lowering her eyes. "I thought you were Jake. He's setting the table."

"Actually," he corrected her, "I sent him upstairs to look in on Sydney. She should be waking up from her nap around now."

She saw that Anderson had come into the kitchen by himself. She looked around, but no one else came in behind him.

"Where's Lexie?" she asked.

"On her way back to the airport," Anderson answered. "Why?"

She shrugged vaguely, feeling progressively more uncomfortable. "I just thought she'd be staying for dinner—that is, unless you thought it might be a little awkward to explain to her what I was doing here."

"Why would it be awkward?" he asked her, confused. "Where else would my wife be but in our house?"

Marina looked at him in surprise. "You told her that we got married?"

It was clear why he didn't understand why she looked so surprised. "Among other things, yes. Why?" Even as he asked, he couldn't come up with a reason why Marina wouldn't want that.

Marina shrugged again, feeling at a loss. "I just thought you wouldn't want her to know."

That obviously cleared up nothing for him. "Correct me if I'm wrong, but wasn't that the initial point of our getting married? I mean, that was why you first made the suggestion, right?"

Why was he making her say this? Making her spell it all out? "Yes, but now that Lexie's moving here, I figured that you wouldn't need to keep up pretenses and telling her might just get her angry."

"Pretenses," he repeated as if he wasn't sure what she was trying to say.

Did he realize that he was torturing her? Marina wondered. "Well, yes."

"But we *are* married, so that's not a pretense."

"No, but—"

Anderson was getting a bad feeling about this. "Are you saying that you don't want to be married?" he asked her point-blank.

"No, I want to be married," she told him. She felt as if her thoughts were getting all jumbled up. "But you don't."

"I don't?" he questioned. What was she talking about?

"No," she cried. Why was he making her say this? Didn't he realize how much it hurt? "I know that the only reason you agreed to marry me was because you needed to prove to the court that you had a stable home environment, with a wife and even a baby, to offer Jake. But now that Lexie's going to be moving to Montana, everything's changed."

"Everything?" he questioned, repeating the word slowly.

"Well, yes. You can be together with Lexie if you want to—"

Anderson stopped her right there. "Oh, Lord, no, why would I want that?"

Marina was completely dumbfounded. "You don't want that?" she asked, bewildered.

He was a man of few words—but more than a few were needed here to fix this. He gave it a try.

"Marina, all I want is to stay married to you and to be a dad to Jake and Sydney. It doesn't matter to me where Lexie is, Chicago or here. You're the one I want, the one I love. I'm not going to force you if you don't want to be married to me, but—"

"Not want to be married to you?" Marina repeated as if he had said something she couldn't begin to comprehend. "Of course I want to be married to you. There's nothing I want *more* than to be married to you. I just didn't want you to feel obligated to continue with this if your heart wasn't in it—"

"My heart," he told her, taking her into his arms, "is exactly where it's supposed to be."

She smiled up into his eyes. "Mine, too."

"Good to know, Mrs. Dalton," he murmured just before he kissed her. "Very good to know."

* * * * *

Get 4 FREE REWARDS!

We'll send you 2 FREE Books plus 2 FREE Mystery Gifts.

FREE Value Over **$20**

Both the **Harlequin® Special Edition** and **Harlequin® Heartwarming™** series feature compelling novels filled with stories of love and strength where the bonds of friendship, family and community unite.

YES! Please send me 2 FREE novels from the Harlequin Special Edition or Harlequin Heartwarming series and my 2 FREE gifts (gifts are worth about $10 retail). After receiving them, if I don't wish to receive any more books, I can return the shipping statement marked "cancel." If I don't cancel, I will receive 6 brand-new Harlequin Special Edition books every month and be billed just $5.24 each in the U.S. or $5.99 each in Canada, a savings of at least 13% off the cover price or 4 brand-new Harlequin Heartwarming Larger-Print books every month and be billed just $5.99 each in the U.S. or $6.49 each in Canada, a savings of at least 20% off the cover price. It's quite a bargain! Shipping and handling is just 50¢ per book in the U.S. and $1.25 per book in Canada.* I understand that accepting the 2 free books and gifts places me under no obligation to buy anything. I can always return a shipment and cancel at any time by calling the number below. The free books and gifts are mine to keep no matter what I decide.

Choose one: ☐ **Harlequin Special Edition**
(235/335 HDN GRCQ)

☐ **Harlequin Heartwarming**
Larger-Print
(161/361 HDN GRC3)

Name (please print)

Address   Apt. #

City   State/Province   Zip/Postal Code

Email: Please check this box ☐ if you would like to receive newsletters and promotional emails from Harlequin Enterprises ULC and its affiliates. You can unsubscribe anytime.

Mail to the **Harlequin Reader Service:**
IN U.S.A.: P.O. Box 1341, Buffalo, NY 14240-8531
IN CANADA: P.O. Box 603, Fort Erie, Ontario L2A 5X3

Want to try 2 free books from another series! Call 1-800-873-8635 or visit www.ReaderService.com.

---

*Terms and prices subject to change without notice. Prices do not include sales taxes, which will be charged (if applicable) based on your state or country of residence. Canadian residents will be charged applicable taxes. Offer not valid in Quebec. This offer is limited to one order per household. Books received may not be as shown. Not valid for current subscribers to the Harlequin Special Edition or Harlequin Heartwarming series. All orders subject to approval. Credit or debit balances in a customer's account(s) may be offset by any other outstanding balance owed by or to the customer. Please allow 4 to 6 weeks for delivery. Offer available while quantities last.

Your Privacy—Your information is being collected by Harlequin Enterprises ULC, operating as Harlequin Reader Service. For a complete summary of the information we collect, how we use this information and to whom it is disclosed, please visit our privacy notice located at corporate.harlequin.com/privacy-notice. From time to time we may also exchange your personal information with reputable third parties. If you wish to opt out of this sharing of your personal information, please visit readerservice.com/consumerschoice or call 1-800-873-8635. Notice to California Residents—Under California law, you have specific rights to control and access your data. For more information on these rights and how to exercise them, visit corporate.harlequin.com/california-privacy.

HSEHW22R2

Get 4 FREE REWARDS!

We'll send you 2 FREE Books plus 2 FREE Mystery Gifts.

Both the **Harlequin® Historical** and **Harlequin® Romance** series feature compelling novels filled with emotion and simmering romance.

Get 4 FREE REWARDS!

We'll send you 2 FREE Books plus 2 FREE Mystery Gifts.

FREE Value Over **$20**

Both the **Romance** and **Suspense** collections feature compelling novels written by many of today's bestselling authors.

Get 4 FREE REWARDS!

We'll send you 2 FREE Books plus 2 FREE Mystery Gifts.

FREE
Value Over
$20

Both the **Harlequin Intrigue®** and **Harlequin® Romantic Suspense** series feature compelling novels filled with heart-racing action-packed romance that will keep you on the edge of your seat.

HARLEQUIN
PLUS

Announcing a **BRAND-NEW** multimedia subscription service for romance fans like you!

Read, Watch and Play.

Experience the easiest way to get the romance content you crave.

Start your **FREE 7 DAY TRIAL** at www.harlequinplus.com/freetrial.